# TERRADOX 2

## The Ranch

R.A. Rex Draco

nXc

Book Cover by R.A. Rex Draco
Illustrations by R.A. Rex Draco

# TIERAN FLAG

# CONTENT WARNING

Bullying
Classism
Religion
Slavery
Death

# CONTENTS

# CHAPTER ONE

## Short Sighted Reach Of The Law

Pandora couldn't believe what he was seeing. The deceased was slammed around like garbage as the doctor lost his temper. The so-called doctor stamped out his patient's life and threw a fit after the fact. His anger didn't stem from the premature death, nor the limitations of medicine. Instead his anger stemmed from their inability to survive the harsh treatment. After throwing the body and his tools scattering across the floor the crow Avius would march forward towards the discarded body which had been thrown so aggressively it had bent and twisted in an awkward manner as it lay against the floor, pushed up against the nearest wall. Pestarz loomed over the body. His claws looked to be bare, no shoes or sandals to be seen. This was important because Pandora could see he wasn't the same and it settled his nerves a bit. Sometimes he worried about the rumors of increased aggression in people during certain lunar tides, but he had never experienced it himself nor knew any other Avius to ask about it. Seeing the way this man was acting one could surmise he was suffering from the lunar cycle. His claws were a much lighter color than Pandora's, almost orange in hue.

The man stepped over the metal tools, seemingly ignoring the pointed, piercing edges of the curved metal, the stabbing hooks, and sharp knives. His talons had hard scales unlike that of other soft-padded Tierans. He would crouch down, pulling his wings over his head as he reached his hand out to grab the unmoving body by its throat.

"Why?" The doctor crowed angrily. "You could have just lived for a little. How could you betray my expectations...?" He blinked his eyes, the only thing visible among the fabric of his hat and raised collar. Even his curved beak barely peeked out of the cloth.

"*Doctor*!" A voice called from outside the room. The doctor raised his head, dropping the body back on the ground. "*We have another patient in the other r-room ready*!" It was the woman from before, her voice still trembling. Moving to wipe his hand on his coat he would stand and walk towards the door. Opening it the Avius would step out.

"Get rid of the body, into the pyre like the rest. It's not worth preserving." Was the last his voice would rumble out before the door closed.

Inside the vent Pandora would feel his body slump and give in to the insurmountable feelings that filled him. Anger, disgust, shock, and outright confusion. How could someone be so cold and cruel? Wasn't the man a doctor? He had a job of which he swore an oath in order to fulfill. He felt himself panting, but his heart couldn't calm enough for him to slow his breath. Mara wasn't sure how to help him. She could see him in distress, but what had she just seen? She couldn't comprehend it herself. To her it looked like the Avius killed the man, having not expected him to survive whatever treatment he was giving and would act anyway. Pandora was in front of her, so all Mara could do was reach out her hands and move to rest them on the man's shoulders. He was startled and looked back at her, but when he realized it was only Mara the man would relax and lean against her, his own wings tightening against his back as if they were melting into his body. He would lean his back against her chest as he tried to think.

"We can't just leave him here..." Pandora thought aloud. "I have to stop him--" As he shifted his weight to stand Mara would pull him back against her chest. Not having expected the action he fell into her lap once more and turned his head to look back over his shoulder.

"And do what?" Mara looked over to Pandora, her deep, orange eyes stared into his green ones. She understood his frustrations. She too wanted to confront this madman, but there was one important thing they were forgetting. "This isn't our village. Not only are we outsiders, I'm a heretic and you're a little monk from a tinier village." Pandora shook his head.

"I can take him down!" He tried to remember their voices carried in the passage and turned to face Mara, standing on his knees. He reached out to grab her face, cupping her cheeks into his hands. "Just leave it to me okay? You can go back to the Eye of Newt and wait for me." He sat there face to face with Mara, his hands still holding her gently despite their trembling. She can feel his anxiousness and desire to stop the man. "I'll drag him outside and pluck all his feathers so he couldn't get away and --" Before Pandora could continue Mara leaned in and pressed her face into his neck. Opening her mouth she would nip down against the side of his neck, causing the Avius to shiver instinctively against the deadly placement of the predator's fangs.

After a moment Pandora would relax and sit back. He moved to tuck his legs beneath him so he could crouch, Mara released her hold and leaned back. "I understand." She would defend. "But who knows how many people are here. If there's a lot of guards... didn't that Gnolus say there were a lot of Orderly here?" Pandora nodded at her words. "Let's head back. We can think of something better to do. I think we should use our heads." Mara was right. Rushing in was a fast way of getting stuffed into a grave in short order.

"...you're right. We'll... think of a plan." He understood the value of planning it seemed and this caused the Drakus' heart to jump in her chest. None of her comrades thought planning was vital to a hunt. They felt acting on instinct and experience was enough. It was why they were so against her plan in the first place, because it took logical planning over outright action into account. "It's better to have a plan in place than have others plan our funerary rites." He motioned his head. "Come on, let's head back." Glad to see he agreed to this much Mara would turn and start back from the way they came.

Once the pair were outside they made their way back to the cart loaned to them by Eye of Newt. Pandora settled in his position behind the handlebar while Mara climbed aboard. They let Miru know of the situation they ran into. She apologized for asking them to check, not realizing how bad it was. The Gnolus stood outside of the hospice and motioned her hand.

"Don't worry dears. I'll look into things and keep you abreast of the situation." She promised. Standing beside her was Gabe and the two would wave the pair off as they departed. She looked over to Gabe and put her finger to her mouth. "You keep this quiet now Gabe. I want to make sure those two stay safe and you do as well. I'm going to talk to the Cleric in the meantime." Gabe blinked his big eyes and gave a salute.

"I understand Miru!"

-

-

-

As the two made their way back down the road towards the Eye of Newt to return the wagon, Pandora's eyes were down along his path. Some people greeted him with reverence while others ignored him completely. Mara leaned against the side of the wagon bed's edge, watching. Her arms were crossed as she rested her head between her limbs. She was thinking for a while and couldn't help but find herself wondering what would have happened had she let Pandora go on his way and stop that mad man.

"Isn't violence against the Oikos' laws?" Mara questioned, her lips brushing up against her arms. This caused Pan to raise his head and glance in her direction, though he didn't fully turn his head. "I mean you're a monk of the order. Shouldn't you be opposed to using violence?"

Pandora smirked, his features straining as he tried not to scowl. "Y-you're right, but that doesn't mean we aren't above defending those in need. While it's suggested to try and talk things out first ... do you think a person like that would have talked?" Mara turned her eyes away, knowing the answer to that question. "I can't stand thinking like that. I'm sure my brothers would be frustrated with me, but I feel sometimes it's better to act rather than sit around and hope someone wants to talk. I don't like that feeling of helplessness." He sighed, knowing he wasn't the most patient monk out there, but he really wanted to dig his talons into that guy's face. "Besides we're trained in Taipau, so it isn't as if I'm helpless, you know?"

Mara sputtered and sat up. "What do you mean Taipau?!" She fell back on her tail and motioned her hands frantically. "Isn't that a super old martial art that can overcome reality and bend things that shouldn't be bent?!" Pandora found himself laughing at her explanation.

"Well when you put it like that -- that's the legend, but Oikos monks have been using the art as a form of meditation for generations. It's why we can defend those in need when we have to as we have the means. Though violence is looked down upon, so is not being able to take care of your brethren, you know? Besides I bet you it's one of those things like with the rainbow bridges. Exaggeration, exaggeration of legends." Mara huffed at his dismissive response and crossed her arms over her chest. "Besides -- oof!"

Pan let out a surprised noise when he bumped into someone. He turned his head only for a moment, but it was long enough to lose sight of the road. When he looked up to apologize he found himself face to face with a familiar figure. It was the spotted lizard he had met the day before. She wore an old shawl over her head and shoulders. Her blouse had long sleeves, but the fabric stopped just above her abdomen, showing off the smooth scales along her sides. Her skirt was tied in place by a dark green sash that contrasted her pale, yellow scales. The skirt was dark brown and her blouse pale tan. Her horns were soft forms, dark yellow nubs peeking out from beneath white hair. From her hip down to her toes she was covered in the same pale scales as well as the top of her arm, likely up to her shoulders. For her kind her tail was rather short and lacked the distinct fatness they were known for, but it was clear she was a type of salamander Salamandrus. The Salamandrus had a wide range of features that were often mistaken for Drakus or Saurus Tierans. What made them stand out were their soft, skin-like scales and semi-aquatic natures.

"Oh, it's you..." Pan recalled her as it was difficult to forget a person who's horns were so soft they could move like ears. He glanced up, watching the soft forms squirm when he spoke. She opened her mouth, but would nod. Mara narrowed her eyes, softly growling at the demure figure. At the sound her horns seemed to twitch as she squeaked and took a step back. "Ah, is there something I can help you with?" The salamander looked over to the Avius and nodded, a serious expression drawing onto her features.

# CHAPTER TWO

## A Prayer A Day

After dropping off the wagon Pandora and Mara would arrive at the church with one another. Mara stood beside Pan, her shoulder almost touching his. In fact every time he tried to move a bit away she inched closer! It was a little confusing for the monk, seeing her behave in such a manner. It was almost like flock behavior or something strange like that. It made him more uncomfortable for her to move away, but it was weird she was acting this way. He would ignore it for now and turned to face the salamander Tieran. When he moved to face her the salamander jumped back. She looked to be on edge, but it wasn't as if he was a predator or some authority figure. It made him sigh a little.

"Rika, was it, right?" Pandora would try to reaffirm his memory. Names weren't difficult, but sometimes he wasn't listening with the intent to remember them. The woman nodded which made him smirk. She was quiet, hardly spoke and when she did it was soft and one had to strain to listen. "Right. So there isn't much I can do on my own. As you can see I'm just a monk of Oikos so this is the best I can do for you."

"Why should you even do this much?" Mara huffed and crossed her arms over her chest. "She isn't a heretic, right?" Most

Salamandrus lived within zones considered outside of heretic territory.

"Yes and no... because Rika here lost her identification." Pandora would explain. "Without it there's a lot of things she won't be able to do on her own. For now, until she can get a new one or find hers, staying at the church is the best. Right?" He looked over to Rika who smiled. Her head was still hidden beneath her hood, but her smile was visible. "Alright let's head inside. Jasper said the Cardinal is who we want to talk to." Pandora would turn. As he moved to enter the church Rika would move to follow, but Mara quickly followed Pandora, getting between her and the Avius.

-

-

-

Inside a small office the Cardinal would meet with Pandora and his two followers. It was a simple room with a desk the Cardinal sat at, a shelf behind him with a few books, and a window to his left which was currently closed over by a blue, velvet curtain. There were two chairs settled in front of the desk leaving Rika to stand as Mara didn't seem to want to be bothered to give up the spot beside Pan. The Cardinal was a type of Avius, though a strange kind that Pan had only ever heard about up until today. The man appeared to have large, round eyes and a small beak. His body was covered in feathers, as he was a kin. Sitting on his beak was a pair of bifocals and he wore white robes with a red sash that was thrown over his shoulders. His small wings were tucked against his sides, the kin's clawed hands folded atop his round belly.

The Avius' main body was covered in brown feathers leaving his head and stomach littered with mottled white and black feathering, at least from what could be seen from around the neck of his collar where he looked to be wearing a thin chain made of silver. Jewelry of some sort it seemed. Pandora had made note of it because the glimmer had caught his eye. The Cardinal frowned a bit and moved to rub the collection of feathers closest to his chin.

"Well seeing as you are looking to help, but..." The Avius cardinal opened an eye and looked the raven Avius over. "... well that's unimportant for now." He mused before pushing to stand. "You can call me Cardinal Hash. I am in charge of the Silver Church. I'm not sure if you've noticed... but we specialize in making silver charms and totems for the shining moon because silver is brightest in the light." He nodded, motioning his hand around.

Indeed just by looking around many of the objects in the room were edged with silver or decorated with silver totems. Silver was quite expensive so this church must receive a lot of donations and be prestigious. But to Pandora it was not impressive, by any means. He felt it was a waste, frivolous. These metals could be used in more constructive manners such as building machines needed by the public, medicine, or even cleaning water. Pandora hated wasteful behavior most of all. The raven would narrow his eyes and click his tongue. Cardinal Hash turned to face him, his thick talons covered in cloth and he had the sort of body one had from a life of leisure. Just what was it that the church members do in their free time?

"Alright," Cardinal Hash began. "I'll show you the daily tasks I expect of you and I'll give you a small allowance so you can use at your discretion! Come come!" So the owl Avius would step out of the office and look around the church's hallway.

The hall led from the main entrance to the offices. To get to the church they had to walk down the opposite way. It was a large building, with a base level and a basement where they kept a mausoleum. The main lobby area had a number of seats for the faithful to occupy at all times of the day and night as the church was never closed. At the front was a totem of their goddess Artimus. Though her physical features were something of an amalgamation of old beliefs and even older paintings from a time where art was more of an abstraction than exact science, it was questionable at best. She looked to be a demi with a beautiful figure and flowing silks over her body. She was said to have the tail of a dragon and the horns of a deer. She had scales on her arms and legs like a fish with the eyes of a serpent. People could come into the church and pray to it whenever they needed. The priests were available most hours of the day, some at night, if ever someone needed a helping hand.

"So," Cardinal Hash began. "We have many rules to our covenant and I will go over them with you as I can, but you should know the basics, the one of not participating in the slaughter of innocents. Not imbibing in alcohol nor participating in gambling. I expect you to avoid those places of vice as well. The red-light district, while a legal house, we of the Artimmus faith look down on the practices of selling one's body." He led the three down the side aisle towards the center of the church where there appeared to be some faithful praying. A few bodies dotted the pews, but it was far from its fullest. Cardinal Hash would notice them looking. He puffed up his feathers proudly. "As you see the seats are not full, many ardents quite independent with their time, but you will see a great number of people arrive until we only have standing room!" He chuckled proudly.

Maybe it was just forgetfulness, but Pandora was sure one of the vices the church considered loathsome, was pride. But nevertheless Pandora would patiently listen, staying mindful of how close Mara was because she had not let up on his personal bubble since they left the hospital. Pandora didn't mind it, but he cleared his throat and looked up, about ready to speak, but noticed Hash looking towards the entrance of the church. There, stepping through the threshold, was the Wolus warrant officer that Pandora and Mara had the misfortune of meeting. He had two men at his side, a stoat Mustus and a rat Rodrus. They looked to be speaking to the Wolus, who leaned to the side, his triangular ear perked in their direction. The kin was looking right at Pandora, Mara standing behind him and glaring past his shoulder. The Wolus smirked and straightened up.

"Well, well, well..." The warrant officer growled. "You found your way to the church after all. I hope the Cardinal will keep you out of trouble, unlike earlier this morning. I heard you had an issue with the Missus of the Pearlescence?" Pandora glanced over to Mara, arching his brow slightly.

"Problem?" Pandora held out his hands. "More of a difference of opinion. She felt I'd make a great addition to her workforce, I disagreed and decided to take a delivery job with the neighboring warehouse." The raven assured.

"Hmph, is that so?" The Wolus didn't like the bird and would rather string him up in the cells with his little Drakus, but he couldn't do so without a valid reason. "Keep your nose clean, boy." He turned to the Cardinal. "But I'm not here for you. Cardinal!" The owl puffed up and turned to face the Wolus. The Cardinal smiled weakly and adjusted the bifocals on his beak. "We heard that a heretic crawled into your church. I'm sure you were thinking of calling us, but we came just in case you had your hands full..." he would chuckle, holding out his paws.

"H-h-heretic!" The Cardinal hooted. "Sir we don't harbour heretics here." He looked over to the Drakus. "This one is ser Pandora's follower if I recall and the other...?" He looked around, but didn't notice where Rika had gone.

"My other follower --" Pandora called out and stepped forward. "Simply misplaced her identification, but she is not a heretic, I can assure you!" He would nod. Rika was peeking around at the group from behind one of the pews. The Wolus curled up his lip, only for Mara to move to stand at Pandora's side, growling.

The warrant officer clenched his fist, cracking his paw's knuckles. "Very well. Don't go picking up the wrong stray, Avius, it'll come back and bite you in the ass. Heretics can't be trusted." He glared at Mara. "They're a traitorous bunch with no faith and will sooner sell you to Slavers for an extra copper than put their necks out for another." He straightened himself up and folded his arms behind his back. "Until later Cardinal.... boy..." He looked between the owl and raven before turning to leave.

"M-m-m..." The Owl shook out his feathers before looking to Pandora. "It seems we have a bit in common ser Pandora." Hash chuckled as he removed his fogged up bifocals to wipe them off using the sash over his shoulders. "Warrant officer Greyfist dislikes us both. A bit of a straight arrow, to the letter of the law, but not to worry. The fact that he is a Artimmus faithful means he keeps the tenants!" But Pandora found that last part hard to believe. Just because one had faith didn't mean they were always true to it...

# CHAPTER THREE

## Mistaken Identity?

There was something that Pandora couldn't shake about that interaction with warrant officer Greyfist. Talking with the man always left him feeling like he had dirt in his eyes and he couldn't stop squinting in disgust and doubt of how the man handled things. His position was probably one secured through power and acts of dominance. He would accept such a thing as probably necessary if they dealt with dangerous people. But Mara wasn't dangerous, nor was Rika! For the time being he put it out of his mind because he had one important thing to focus on and it was the strange things happening in the hospital. He had plans to make with Mara, but now he also had Rika to help.

"Cardinal Hash?" Pandora clasped his hands together and lowered his body slightly. This way he didn't seem as if he was trying to be an upstart or cause trouble. The submissive motion was also something used to appease those in higher positions. Frankly, Pan couldn't stand it. He didn't feel comfortable doing such things, or did it feel natural. Even with his brothers they didn't seem to have a hierarchy. While brother Bryne was the head monk, they were so by seniority and their experience at the Hale's monastery. "I wanted to ask you something, about what the warrant officer had said." Cardinal Hash would come to a stop in front of a supply closet. He scratched the side of his head and blinked his large eyes.

"Well, I don't know how I can help... ha ha, the officer is quite strict, but he doesn't come around here a lot." Talk of the warrant officer didn't sit right with Hash. He tried his best to keep the curiosity of the officers out of the church's business. "It's best he doesn't come around the church since some of our edicts contradict with his view of the law." Which, to Pan, didn't make too much sense hearing it out loud. Shaking his head Pandora raised his hand, dismissing the thought.

"No, no. I was just curious about something you told him." He'd reassure the Cardinal. "You said you don't take in heretics?" This confused Pandora because it was usually the duty of the faithful to restore the faith of a heretic. He wasn't sure exactly how it worked for the Artimmus' faith, but now was a good time to find out.

"Oh," Cardinal Hash chuckled softly, understanding the confusion he had. "Yes, yes. We do not take in heretics because we are a church, not a sanctuary. We help build places like hospieces or rehabilitation centers to restore the faith in the lost or teach heretics so they can learn to become true faithful, but it would be problematic for the government if our buildings were used for such a case. We are specially built to sanction handfastings, to settle the faithful, and exorcisms, though," He would chuckle thinking about it. "We haven't had an official exorcism in centuries." He would clap his hand at the amused thought. "But beyond that, were we to ever act as a sanctuary and house heretics we would lose our protection from the government to participate in the education of the community, our printing and selling of the religious doctrine would be banned, and we could no longer participate in local politics as people would be afraid we would push agendas in favor of heretics."

All in all this place tried its best to survive in an environment that inherently shunned heretics for the threats they brought to a large city space. Perhaps it was because he was privileged to be able to be in a place where he could help others freely, or where their acts of kindness impacted him in ways he could not easily forget, but he felt this church was too cowardly. They were too interested in maintaining a status quo rather than saving people. Even still he would be depending on these people for his survival for the next few days, or at least until he could save enough to regularly get himself and Mara meals. But now he also had to account for Rika! Speaking of...

"Hey Mara, did you see where Rika went?" Pandora asked, while Cardinal Hash collected some work clothes for the two. Mara curled up her lip at the question. The raven Tieran pulled the corner of his lip up as he chuckled nervously. Luckily Cardinal Hash had his back turned from the vicious looking Drakus. He wasn't sure what had her up in arms but he moved to reach out his hand and touch the side of her face. "I was hoping you were keeping an eye out while I was talking to the Cardinal..." She furrowed her eyes at the touch and tried her best not to turn her gaze and snap at the hand that would be feeding her. Mara would sneer, but give in. Letting her shoulders sink she sighed.

"I -- she's hiding over there." Turning her head she would expose Rika's hiding spot, very much to the Salamandrus' surprise. She had thought she crept away when the two were preoccupied, but she hadn't even noticed the Drakus' woman watching her. Usually people ignored her as she did well to keep her distance. Her quiet nature and unassuming figure was sometimes a blessing as much as it was a curse. Because she was a bit on the short side and her figure was a little round, almost chubby, she was seen as soft and demure, someone who didn't cause trouble. "Why? She's not your real follower, is she?" She was just a temporary member of Pandora's following. "Not that I care, mind you, it's just more mouths you'll have to feed." In that sense Pandora could understand why she may have been bothered. They would have to do more work.

"Well that's fine. We'll help her out and she can be on her way and that way we can talk about our other problems." He wanted to deal with that as soon as possible. Meanwhile Cardinal Hash turned around and handed the two of them some clothes. "What's this Cardinal?" When he was given a folded pack of clothing he would note that it looked similar to his clothing, with a few key differences, such as the length of the sleeves and pants. But he had clothes and they covered his body well. The owl Avius turned around and smiled warmly.

"Those are for the girls." He moved to rest his claws on his stomach and closed his eyes in a smile. "Unfortunately in Artimmus, we are expected to cover as much of our bodies as possible." It would explain why even his talons had covers over them. "Though you are of Oikos and are probably a little more frugal and simple with your clothing, we operate in larger communities that have different cultures and not all of our followers find exposing the body as a positive expression. So I'll expect you to wear those while you work within the church or whenever you are running tasks for us. Now I'll show you to the room you'll be staying in with your followers." Cardinal Hash would turn and lead them to the sleeping quarters for the church's priests. "Now these rooms are shared so you're expected to keep it tidy. Now we never have had anyone staying there on a semi-permanent status since our priests have their own homes. I suspect you will only be staying until you can get your own place..." He clapped his claws together when they arrived in front of the rooms. "Alright, I shall leave things to you. I will see you after lunch and send you on your first duties." The Cardinal would turn to leave.

Rika was peeking around the corner at the end of the hall when Cardinal Hash made himself scarce. Pandora would wave her down and the three would enter the room. It had a number of cots laid out end to end. At the end of each cot was a footlocker where a person could store away personal effects. When Rika entered the room after Mara and himself he would hand her some of the clothing.

"So I wanted to ask Rika," Pandora began as the Salamandrus selected a bed and set her clothes down to look through them. Mara remained by his side as he had yet to pick a spot to settle. "Your Identification, what happened to it?" He reached down into the front of his shirt and pulled out his loop of shells, showing how they were normally kept. "Yours were tied up like this as well, right?" Rika frowned, but nodded.

She moved her hands as she spoke, fingers looking to move in complicated motions as she talked in her quiet voice. "It was an accident." She'd admit. "Lost it at the markets when helping unload the ships. I'm not very strong so I dropped some stuff. They got mad at me and hit me. I lost it after. I'm glad the monk is helping me..." She would smile. Mara didn't like it though. How could this girl lose something so important and take on a task that was beyond her ability? Pan finally picked a bed and Mara moved to settle on the cot beside the one he chose. Pandora stared at her and opened his mouth to speak, but thought better of it. He was sure he could guess it was flock behavior. Drakus are the kind to hunt in groups so he didn't want to upset her and make her think he didn't want her around.

But what he wasn't quite aware of was that it was a little more than just a tendency to gang together that Mara was displaying. After getting into the garbs given to them by the Cardinal the three would take a rest before heading to lunch with the clergy.

# CHAPTER FOUR

## Clearing The Junk

The midday meal was an awkward affair for all involved. Though they broke bread together, the clergy members acted quite differently depending on their position within the clergy. Every member had years of experience that was sometimes overshadowed by natural talent. There was a stifling sense of competition among the clergy that Pandora had never experienced with his brothers. It seemed more of a contest than anything else.

The church had a few roles that were easily recognized by the public space. First there were the Priests who had just finished their training and could publicly work to spread the faith and offer practitioners prayers. Next were the Bishops who spent ten years learning every rite in their doctrine and could now act independently to carry on these rites without the oversight of a Cleric or Cardinal. Then there were the Cardinals who acted as leaders of their church and a had little over thirty years of experience. Finally there were Clerics. This was the highest honour the church offered individuals who have shown exceptional duty to the faith. There are only three known Clerics with one residing in Mene while the other two lived outside the city.

Pandora had chosen to sit at the end of the long table while the groups conversed and spouted off about people they have been working with or someone they managed to save or bring into the faith. This was something he had to also think carefully about. Brother Bryne had talked about how he had to convert people back to Okios, to bring heretics into the faith in order to maintain the world, yet it seemed an impossible task at first glance. This church sounded like they struggled to even maintain those they had.

"Yes well while you were fooling around in the slums one of the Grassjumpers felt our devotion was lacking because of your focus. They are considering other faiths or even departing!" The priests went back and forth concerning their daily dilemmas.

"It wouldn't be so troublesome if these new false faiths didn't keep cropping up. Isn't it the Bishops' job to see this from happening since they're out there working?!" There looked to be a need for cooperation despite the divide.

All the while Pandora listened and ate. Though the church's table was full Pandora chose to eat little, not feeling his appetite among the figures. Mara sat at his side and fully took advantage of having a plate of food. Personally she felt the food at the Eye at Newt tasted better in many ways. After dropping off the wagon they had a meal with them before arriving at the Church, and there had been no such arguments... Afterwards Cardinal Hash would call for Pandora and his followers to his office.

"So ser Pandora, as you see there are quite a number of us here at the church." Cardinal Hash would explain. "With Mene being such an active city, we're kept quite busy." The man brushed his claws against his robes to smooth them down. "We have some garbage we'd like you to take to the dump. It'll help us out immensely." The Cardinal paused and motioned his claw, his wing brushing against his robes as he moved. "Of course you'll be fairly compensated for this task." Hearing he would get a reward made Pandora sit up a bit. "Everything's been collected in the back of the kitchen, you and your cohorts merely need to collect everything and head out." With that Pandora, with Mara at his side, made his way to the back of the kitchen where a mountain of trash had been gathered by the back exit.

"What in the --?" Pan moved to rest his fists on his hips as he stared at the pile with a measure of disgust. "Those who don't waste, find fortune..." He muttered as he looked over to Mara who had a similar look on her face. "Sorry to ask, but do you mind helping?" She rolled her eyes and turned her head away.

"It isn't like I've much choice since they all expect me to do things with you..." She wanted to simply say no. It wasn't as if she was obligated to help.

"Well, you're not obligated to help, but it would be nice. Two hands makes the work go faster. By the way, have you seen Rika?" She had once again disappeared and he was so deep in his thoughts concerning the hospital and the unsettling feelings he had in a new environment that he hadn't bothered to pay attention. It wasn't as if he was Rika's keeper.

"As if--" She growled. "She left after eating. I saw her go out to the hall while everyone was still bickering." For her it was an unusual meal time. She much preferred the company of the Eye of Newt's workers because they knew how to talk to a lady and discussed foraging their plants rather than who convinced who to follow which goddess. "Why?" She was curt in her questioning because it was all she wanted to know. Why did he need to know where Rika was?

"Why?" It was a valid question. "Well I would rather not stress out thinking about that warrant officer. He has it out for me so if Rika's wandering around without her identification and I claimed responsibility for her -- well..." It was safe to assume the officer would arrest her for loitering or something benign just to do it. Realizing that was indeed the case, Mara became more alert. There was no telling what that woman was up to. Mara didn't trust her. Pandora would chuckle at her sudden attentiveness before he moved to open the back exit. He propped the door open with a heavy block put aside for just that very purpose and began carrying out the containers of trash one by one. Pandora piled the crate containers one atop the other before he looked to the end of the church's alley.

"Oh! Rika!" Pan had turned his head up and noticed the little salamander standing with her hands tugging at her shawl's hood and a wide eyed look. It seems she wasn't expecting Pandora to be there. She looked behind her, then in front of her before turning her attention to Pan. She began to move her hand, opening her mouth, but remembered to speak.

"When did you come outside?" Her hands appeared to move when she spoke, sometimes miming her words. "Is he doing a job?" Her voice was incredibly low that if Pandora wasn't looking at her face he would sometimes miss her words, the male sometimes having to follow her lips' movements.

"Oh, yeah. We're going to the dump to drop off this trash, though I need to ask the Cardinal where it is... first I want to collect everything to make it easier to carry. Are you gunna help?" He hoped he'd have another pair of hands because the amount of trash this clergy collected was twice what his village used to collecting in the span of a week. Much of their trash was reused and any uneaten food was composted for gardens.

"Yes!" Rika moved her hand and pointed back. "I know a place to get a map! I'll be right back!" She seemed to brighten up before turning to hurry away, her little tail flailing behind her. Pandora watched as she hurried off before he looked behind him as Mara dropped down a large armful of crates, chuckling a bit at her impressive moving power.

-

-

-

Rika hurried through the streets towards the docks. She made sure to stick to the side roads where more civilians walked, leaving the nosy officers to their patrols near the shoppes and ships. The Salamandrus slowed from her hurried waddles to a stable walk as her three wide, padded toes pressed silently against the concrete roads. She clutched the front of her shawl, trying to hide her features before she tucked down between some of the stacked cargo towards a certain docked vessel.

"Look who we have here boys..." The deep, rumbling voice called cooly. Rika came to a stop and turned her head up towards the top of the vessel where stood a black Wolus with an eye patch. "Did you find my quarry lass?" Rika looked around before she moved to write in the air using her hands, the woman unable to find her voice. "Oh?" It seemed the Wolus followed her fingers and was able to read her non-verbal speech. "It seems our little Cardinal is trying to keep our little birdie for himself. And what do you need from us, blue tongue?" Rika's lips pursed, glancing away. "Aww I didn't mean it disrespectfully. Come on, it isn't like you owe them anything. We're the ones that brought you here free of charge, right?" She would hesitate, but moved her hands. "Is that all you need?" He chuckled before turning his head to whistle.

Down on the ground another black Wolus, a member of the crew, would approach the salamander with a piece of folded paper. Rika would take the paper and open it, revealing a small map with the local dump circled. She looked up to the Wolus who smirked. She would frown and move her fingers through the air, touching her finger to her chest at the end of her words.

"Oh you have my word." The black Wolus grunted. "Not a scale on your tail'll be touched. We just want the bird and dragon." He swore. "And I'll give you what it is you want. The identification right? We have plenty to give!" He chuckled. "But you only got an hour, girl. Get them to the dump and wait. Got it?" He snapped his jaws at her before Rika jumped and turned to run off. The black Wolus moved to lean his arm on the edge of the ship, looking down at his man who had given her the map. "Take two others with you and follow her. I don't trust those slimy lizard wannabes." The Wolus below would salute and hurry. "He he he... An eye for an eye birdie...." he tapped his eye patch.

# CHAPTER FIVE

## Identifying The Threat

Rika was glad it hadn't cost anything to get the map from the Slavers. She had nothing left to give in this case. It had been hard enough securing a spot on a ship that was going anywhere. To think, though, it was coming here to the Capital. She was even more surprised the captain of the Slaver ship knew how to read handtalking. There wasn't anyone in her village except her mother who could read her handtalking so when her mother died she was unable to really get along well with people in the village since she could not hear what they were saying unless she was looking at their mouths. Even though her speaking was quite good, her tribe had found it troublesome to always talk to her face and constantly feeling the whispers behind her back was difficult.

"There you are!" Rika would get pushed from her solemn thoughts when she noticed the raven Avius call out to her. Looking up Rika would smile and hold out her hand, waving. She would open her mouth as if to speak, but taking notice of Mara glancing at her from the side she would lower her hand and hug the map to her chest. "Were you able to find a map?" As Rika walked over towards Pandora she held out the paper, pointing down to the circled location. "Is this it?" He would look over the shapes in excitement. From where he remembers the church to be at they were quite a bit aways from the dump. "Ah..." He sighed. "Well at least there's three of us." He chuckled, looking over to the two women. Mara glanced over to Rika, looking a bit displeased, but Rika, on the other hand, seemed eager!

It wasn't long after that that the trio were on their way. Pandora had locked his pack up tight in the footlocker at the church while he did this task. He decided to tie some of the crates together to carry on his back in a manner similar to how he would his knapsack. He helped Mara tie up some crates together and they both helped Rika, though her load was much smaller. With everything rounded up the trio made their way to the dump which was a good ten minute walk from the docks. When they arrived at the dumping ground it appeared to be a massive lot of open land bordered by a metal fence similar to what he saw at the Pearlescence. Mounds of garbage created hills from their mass alone. Some have been pounded flat by heavy rollers pulled across the patches by beast and cart. A few were currently busy at the task in question. Rika walked up towards Pan and tapped his shoulder to get his attention. When Pan looked over she began to move her hand.

"I am sure my identification is here. It was thrown away." She pointed to one of the piles and looked back to Pandora as she moved her hand, speaking her words. By now Pandora guessed she must move her hands when she speaks out of some sort of habit. "The piles of trash are brought here at certain times of day, in a cycle, weekly." So each mound was a certain day of the week. The one she pointed to was the one from yesterday's refuse collection.

"That's great!" Pandora would nod and walk over towards the gates. "Excuse me..." He looked up towards the booth that stood beside the sealed doors. There a fellow looked to be standing with his elbow leaning onto the counter with his face rested in his hand. In his other hand there appeared to be a magazine. The man was a kin by the looks of his long muzzle. He had a blue cap atop his head and he wore a pair of coveralls. His mouth looked to be full of sharp teeth as his jaw hung open as he read. He had a long, fleshy tail that could be seen peeking out of the opening of the stall. His body was covered in a patchy brown and grey fur, but his muzzle and paws specifically were completely bare of any hair leaving them a clear pink skin. He looked up when Pandora called out to him. "Are we allowed to enter and dump our trash... maybe even look around?"

"Ah! A bit ah treasure huntin' are ya boy? There's plenty ah goodsta find out in'ere an'." He would chuckle before closing his magazine and pressing the gate button. "Real connoisseur ah? But be ere'careful now." The gate operator warned. "You won'tnah just find trash out'ere. Sometimes there's the unlucky soul whatta falls victim to heretic activity, nah, and gets'ah dumped out 'ere. If'n yah find ah body, just give a holler. Gotta report it'nah to ah law." With that the kin waved them off. Pandora, Mara, and Rika would enter the city's dump and begin their search for Rika's identification. They dumped the trash from the church, leaving them burden free.

Mara hopped along the piles of trash with ease. Her harder scales didn't have a problem perusing the piles which had everything from broken wood to discarded sheets of metal. From what Pandora understood, metal in the city was a valuable resource, but seeing them throw pieces away that looked to be a bit broken or bent instead of trying to make use of them by having a smith melt them down into ingots was incredibly wasteful. It was no different than the church's trash which had an immeasurable amount of paper and silver shards. With his legs being covered in scales it was also easy for him to climb across the mounds without hurting himself, but Rika was a different case. Because her scales were so soft she couldn't wade around the dump like they could, but she wouldn't need to. She would only have to distract them for an hour. They already wasted time getting here, but that was still a long time to dig around in garbage. What could she do to delay them?

"What does it look like?" Mara stood atop a pile with her hands on her hips. She had no idea what she was looking for. Identification could be a lot of things. It ranged from bones to even bits of colored cloth. What she hoped they wouldn't find was a body. She was sure none of them they would find came from the hospital since she recalled hearing the man said he burned them. It would be unsettling to run into any that could possibly be sick. "I mean what kind of identifiers do Salamandrus use...?" She wasn't even sure where they were from to try and guess. Mara watched as Pan hopped along the junk, his agility showing off as he was able to leap bounds she wouldn't be able to do herself. Though he was only a little taller than her he didn't seem to have any muscle on his body which gave him an agile and lightweight form.

"Well if I remember..." Pandora would use his claw to pull away some of the layers of junk. "Salamandrus live near islands with the thermal geysers. I heard their territories are popular for tourists because of the healing properties of their warm water." He heard this from Sinclair when he was younger. The brother had gone there for his pilgrimage and learned many things about water he never understood despite living near and around it all his life. Leave it to the mole to have a progressive experience when near a place known for being a spot of relaxation. "One of my brothers visited the villages at the hot springs a long time ago and told me they use the colored stones that are found all over their beaches." Rika would turn to face Pandora and move her hand along the side of her face as a confused look drew a frown on her features.

"How did you know...?" She would point at Pandora as she spoke, her words almost a whisper. Pan tilted his head and surmised by her expression she wasn't sure how he came upon the knowledge himself. "My people they --..." Though her voice faded into silence her hand finished its motion.

[...isolated...]

"Oh, well the brother showed me photos of the place. He's a bit strange, but enjoys looking at pictures of the land and sometimes spends the time it takes to take a photograph or paint it." He always found it a strange hobby of his but because he would always take the time to tell him a story about the place or explain in detail the different things he saw, Pandora always defended the hobby against the other brother's teasing. Quite fervently! Understanding Rika would not, brushing off the thoughts that came with his admittance. Yes she would agree that her home was beautiful, but sometimes the ugliness in people made it difficult to handle. Suddenly she would feel her horns start to twitch. She could feel footsteps. It wasn't time for the Wolus captain to arrive, so who was that?

"Ah, it's just like the captain said! They got thrown out!" The barking laughter of men could be heard in the distance. Pandora, Mara, and Rika turned their heads towards the three figures. Three large Wolus males stood atop one of the larger piles of trash. The one at the front was a lithe looking male with black fur. The kin had a thick mane of fur on his head that was white in color and he appeared to wear the customary garb of his team. Around his chest was a leather harness that held up his pauldrons and supported the holsters at his hips. He wore loose grey pants as did the other two men. The other two appeared to be demi and had a similar uniform, but unlike the kin they wore shirts beneath their harness that appeared to have various markings drawn over them. "Looks like we get to pick up something nice for the ride back!" The sound of ringing metal could be heard as chains were handled. The two demi in the back, with their black, bushy tails, seemed to sway them in excitement as they pulled their lips back in a wide grin, holding the chains and manacles in hand.

# CHAPTER SIX

## Changing Of Colors

The silver-haired kin smirked and focused his eyes on Pandora. He'd never seen a Tieran like him before. His feathers were as dark as the night sky and his legs were strong and sturdy. Though his body was a bit thin, that was something easily fixed with plenty of bread and beer. It was no wonder why his boss was so interested in having him. He'd be sold for top coin. Any collector with sense could see how special he was. It made the kin salivate at the thought of the commission. And he was given leadership for this hunt to catch him?! It was too exciting!

"You two get the girls!" The kin let out howling laughter as he jumped from the pile and slid down the side of the trashy covered hill. He didn't wear boots that covered his digitigrade paws, but instead guards that easily served his purposes as he made his way to the bottom of the slope. As soon as his paws hit the ground he would kick off the uneven surface and take off running towards Pandora.

"Pan!" Mara shouted out. The raven Avius looks to have frozen in the face of such an aggressive predator. She looked to the side, the ringing of the metal intensifying as it drew nearer to her. One of the demi had dismounted from their perch and came charging at her with the intent to clap her in chains, but in no way would she allow that, not after everything. As soon as the demi came close enough she jumped back and swung out her tail as she spun around, turning her back to him. As her tail lashed out towards his chest he would grab his chains at both ends and pull taut, blocking the strike. In order to do so, though, he had to halt his forward charge. When he lowered his chains Mara had started down the discarded pile of garbage and towards Pandora. It wasn't until she was a few feet from him that his eye glanced in her direction.

"Don't worry about me." The raven Avius lowered his stance and would duck as the kin launched passed him, the attempt to grab the bird thwarted by his faster than expected reaction. The silver-haired Wolvus dropped to all fours and slid along the rough surface. "You missed!" The kin stood to his feet and reached to his hip for the whip he had holstered, but when he went to grab it he would find that it was gone. Whorling around he turned to the Avius only to find he was standing on one leg with the whip tightly held in the leg curled close to his chest. "But you should start worrying about yourself."

The last demi made his way towards Rika. He grinned and raised his chain above his head and swung it around as he rushed her. The whistling sound grew louder and louder. Rika had her back turned to the demi, having tried to get the kin's attention, but he charged in before she could get him to explain. What had he meant get the women, there was only the Drakus and --

~B O O W S H~

The chain wielding demi slammed his weapon down. It struck the ground with such force that the metal debris responded with his chain and sparked, throwing the lit embers outward. The demi stared at the spot in front of him. Where had the Salamandrus gone? Having felt his movements behind her the salamander made a quick escape further into the dump. She pulled a piece of wood over her head and crouched down in a secluded spot among the piles.

"Out -- of the **way**!" Mara snarled as she stamped her foot into the back of the demi desperately searching for Rika. The grunt let out a pained shout as he stumbled forward and roughly hit the ground. He rolled forward once before pushing to his feet, dragging the chain. Holding it between both his hands he moved to leave a longer portion loose near his left fist.

"You stay outta mine! Not like the little slimy slut needs your protection! She sold you out!" The demi grinned. "But since you wanna keep me company!" He whipped back the chain before throwing it forward. He was experienced in treating the weapon like a whip despite its size. The chain shot out and went straight for the Drakus.

"What do you mean sold us out?!" Mara moved to strafe to the side, the chain clipping against the side of her arm. "Augh!" Luckily the long sleeves of the church's gaudy garbs hid her scales beneath so the demi wasn't aware he struck armored skin. She dropped to a knee, pretending to be in pain. It did hurt somewhat, but not severely enough to really endeavour her to flinch.

"Haa?!" The kin was surprised he was pickpocketed so easily. "Clever bird, but you won't be clever for long when I knock you enough times upside your head!" But he had to be careful because the kid was product. "What? You think we found you on accident? Who do you think told us where you'd be? And such a great place to bloody you up, you know? The law doesn't come around here!" He cracked his knuckles and charged at Pandora. Looking around, Pandora would realize he couldn't see Rika anywhere. But if Rika was their informant then why were they targeting her too? The black Wolus kin knew the little monk didn't know how to use the whip so he would lunge towards Pandora, but once again the raven Avius moved to the side, evading the kin, his slashing claws barely brushing past the feathers of his wings. It looked as if the bird would take off, but Pandora jumped back and slammed his raised foot on the floor as he moved forward, sending the whip outward. The tail of the whip would end up tangling around one of the kin's legs as he was able to jump up in time to pull his other leg up and prevent both legs from getting lashed together. Taking two steps back he stopped to look at the raven who smirked. "What the --?"

The demi whose attack was stopped by Mara would finally catch up with her and grab both ends of his chain before swinging it out like a bat in an attempt to lash her across the back. Mara caught the movement, the loud chains making it easy to sense their action before they made it. With another clattering ring from the chains Mara would jump up as they came down, turning her body as she pulled her legs up. She outstretched her right leg in order to send a violent kick across his jaw, but she was unable to make contact as he pulled back the chain in time to wrap it around her leg and force her to the ground. The second demi took his chance and as soon as the Drakus was down he raised his chains and would bring it down over her body, striking.

~C R A T Z~

The metal links struck with enough force that any metal surrounding them sparked, lighting up the ground. When the Wolus pulled back the length of weapon he would find the Drakus had pulled her arms over her head, blocking the attack with her arms. He grinned, sure he broke her arms, but when the fabric tore away from her limbs it was revealed her arms were covered in scales. Hard scales, at that. She pulled her bound leg back, which jerked the demi forward. Her knee would bend up and thrust into the underside of his jaw with a crack. The man quickly lost consciousness. The chains around her ankle became loose and she pulled her hands over the crumbling man's back, climbing over him before she lunged at the other, her hands snapping around his throat.

"B-but how!?" he choked out under her grip. "Why do you ha---kgh!" Mara squeezed her hands tighter as she moved to force him to his knees.

"You can thank my father for the scales on my arms!" Mara pulled him further down before she yanked him towards her and slammed her knee into his collarbone, breaking it. The man blacked out. "Now where is that lousy salamander..." She hissed and moved to search around the area. While Mara went on her hunt Pan continued to face down the kin.

"Just give up and let me take you and your cute girls away." The kin Slaver chuckled. "I'll be sure to get you sold off to the same master, or at least near one another at least! Ha!" He roared out and jumped towards the raven. He raised his arms over his head, muscles bulging under the tension of his flex. He clasped his hands together before moving to slam down onto the bird with both speed and power. "Die!"

"You know I'm not in a good mood...." When it came to hand to hand combat Pandora had confidence. He spent his life at the Monastery training in the martial arts day in and day out. When the black Wolus came sailing down Pan would reach up to grab the whip still coiled around his leg and would yank on it before he threw his fist up and swung between the kin's legs.

~CRONCH~

The Wolus crumpled to the floor, slowly sliding off the hill into a pile of trash. Shaking his wrist Pan brushed his hands together and sighed. He would pull his legs up one by one to stretch them. It was difficult for him to walk around in the garbage, though his scales are tough, they weren't impenetrable. He lived his life in a village where the hardest thing he came across was river stones. But where was Mara? Suddenly Pandora heard a strangled shout carry through the air. Worried for Mara he rushed out towards the sound, only to find the Drakus was holding down the Salamandrus by her legs as she struggled to get away.

"Mara! Stop!" Pan would hurry through the garbage, occasionally sinking into the deeper parts of loose trash. He rushed to the

Drakus' side and moved to grab her wrist. Mara rolled her shoulder roughly in an attempt to knock Pan off while keeping hold of her prey.

"Get off me! I'll skin her!" Mara fought to hold onto the flailing salamander, her soft scales making it difficult to find a grip. Pandora would push Mara aside as Rika scrambled to hide herself behind Pandora.

"Mara! Look, I understand you're upset but Rika isn't a bad person, I mean there must be a reason!" He wanted to keep the peace and make sure Mara didn't kill another person for no reason. "Mara, please, let's just hear her out...?" Mara would growl.

"Fine! Keep her until she kills you in your sleep!" She shouted and turned to stomp off. Pandora reached out, but she would leave them behind. Pandora slumped his shoulders and sighed.

# CHAPTER SEVEN:

## A Leg Up In The Right Direction

Pandora and Rika were left there in the dump standing among the garbage after taking out the trash that were the Slavers. The raven Avius felt his arms sink at his sides. He understood that Mara felt uncomfortable with Rika, but there wasn't proof the woman had done any of what the Slavers had said. For all he knew they were saying all those things in order to pit them against one another in a desperate moment. If Mara had hurt, or killed Rika, he would have no choice but to send her away, probably straight to law enforcement. Even though she would have deserved it he didn't want to even think about having to do that. He had saved her because deep down he knew she was a good person that deserved a chance. Why did it feel so bad to see her stalk off like that? He turned his attention to Rika who moved her hand in a certain motion. Pandora canted his head before turning fully in order to face the woman. She would repeat the motion, but this time speak her words in order to express herself.

"I'm sorry." Rika looked over to Pandora who seemed a little downtrodden by the whole situation. The salamander looked up to the raven, her eyes trying to find the right expression to fully endear herself to him. What could she say that would make something like this alright? "She was right," Her hands moved as slowly as she spoke, as if she was carefully picking her words. "I was helping them, but it isn't like I hate you, or her. They helped me leave my home, and I had to pay them back. They asked me to bring you far away." Pandora shook his head, understanding Mara was right to worry. He had foolishly put his neck out for the woman, but he was also not wrong. Rika needed help, just not in the way he thought.

"It was wrong, you know?" Pan wanted to admonish her, but he could understand she probably felt like she owed the Slavers a great deal. Traveling was an expensive commitment and tremendous ordeal. It was probably one of the main reasons people were attacked on ships. They would pack everything they owned and would leave without the intention of ever going back. He was going back home, eventually, but he understood that it was difficult to leave. "Rika, I ..." Mara had mistrusted Rika from the get go and he was dismissive of that fact.

"I know." She moved her hand near her chest. "I'm sorry." Her gentle voice would sound as if it was trying to soothe the man, but she was more distraught than anything else. "I don't have an excuse. It was wrong." Pandora stared off towards the dump's entrance. His body felt a little heavy. Mara had been sticking to his side so much that he thought he would feel relieved that she was gone. He raised his gaze to Rika, leveling himself a bit so he didn't look so dismayed. He stared at her face, the woman wholly expecting for him to slap her.

"I want to ask... Did you mean it when you asked me for help?" Pandora remembered when he first came upon Rika when they first arrived in the city, he was with Mara, looking for a place for the night. Many people approached him that day, but there was something about Rika that had stood out to him. Maybe it was her little spotted tail, perhaps it was her soft voice, but Pan remembered her. "You asked me if I could help you." He placed his hand to his chest. "You asked if I could help you pray that you could find a place to belong...." Rika opened her mouth, surprised of all the people he probably met that day, that he remembered her request.

Back beyond the perimeter of the dumping ground, Mara stood with her shoulder leaned up against the junker's stall. He had set his magazine aside and moved to rest his arms crossed on his counter. The Drakus had stormed out of the dump in a huff. He could guess that a few different things had happened that set the little miss off and caused her to storm out of the treasure trove of a delve such as his dump.

"Ay'nah lil miss. Did ye have'ye ah fight wit'ya boy? Ah, don't take it to heart none, nah? He's excited nah ta have somethin' new, but ain't'he bring ye 'ere? Means somethin' more'an ya think sher!" Mara felt herself frown. Not only was the kin's accent difficult to decipher, but maybe it was just this frustrated feeling in her chest. Couldn't the man just mind his own business. "You know, we ain't always ta be together. Best ta do what we can nah or else we'll 'ave us regrets." Mara slowly turned her head to look in the man's direction. He pulled his lips back over his muzzle in a warm smile. Mara would slowly nod, understanding a bit better. "Ah, 'ere they come nah." The garbage loving kin leaned back as Mara stood up away from the stall. There Mara would see Pandora leaving the gates. She seemed to brighten up, but quickly deflated when she spotted Rika following him out.

"Mara!" Pandora was surprised to see that she was still there, but he then realized that she probably couldn't go back to the church without him. She wouldn't look his way. "R-right." He wasn't sure what he was thinking so he would turn to the stall attendant and wave. "Thank you, sorry if there was any trouble." With that Pandora would start off. Rika came to a stop and looked over to Mara. She hesitated, thinking the woman would have pushed to walk in front of her, but when she didn't the salamander hurried to stick close to Pan after Mara's earlier assault. Mara followed soon after.

They returned to the Church, no worse for the wear, but the

group seemed a little disjointed. Try as he might Pandora couldn't get Mara to respond to his comments. He felt a little sad.

"Ah! Our intrepid heroes! Hoho !" The old owl Avius chuckled in jest. "I see you completed your task well! Not a bit of trash was left behind!" He was glad they were so quick with their work. With as much trash that was there he thought they'd be gone longer. Blinking his eyes the Avius would notice something in the air between the three. He wasn't sure what was off but pressed on. "Well come now let's put you to work!" The Cardinal pursed his beak, but would nod and turn on his pads before heading out of his office.

Pan would look back in hopeful excitement at the two, but when his eyes came upon them they didn't have the faces he expected. Rika was smiling softly, but she had a sad expression as she stood two arm lengths from Mara. Mara had her head turned away, a frown on her face as she seemed to be distancing herself from the situation as she kept her arms crossed over her chest.

First Cardinal Hash would have the three help with gathering dinner supplies from the larder for the kitchen. Pan was familiar with the task so took it on with gusto, hoping to encourage the mood of his entourage. Pandora moved the first crate of vegetables down from the rest and went ahead to collect some root bulbs for seasoning. Rika wanted to help so she went to collect the crate of veggies only to struggle with its weight.

"Oh, Rika let me carry that! You can take the bulbs!" The raven would chuckle before he turned towards Mara. "Do you mind taking the barrel--" As he looked up the Drakus had already hoisted the barrel he moved aside over her shoulders and left to take it to the kitchen. "*...of wine, yeah...*" his voice finished in a soft, disappointed tone. Mara did exactly what was expected of her, but Pandora hoped she would be a little uncooperative...

Mara herself wasn't sure what to do. She thought deeply about the junker's words. She wasn't sure how much time she had with

Pandora, but she was sure he preferred someone with softer scales and acted more feminine. Drakus females were warriors and particularly dominant in their culture. Though male and female were generally equal in the Drakus culture, women and those who were feminine in their nature were the ones that cared for the young so they were fiercer in order to guard their family nests.

"...*Pan wouldn't want to have an egg with me*." Mara whispered to herself. She knew she was rough around the edges. Sometimes she was teased for being too masculine, but she liked cute things and wanted to be soft too, but being the runt of her family she had to be tough. By the time Mara arrived in the kitchen, Pan and Rika were making their way down the hall.

"...are you okay monk?" Rika looked to Pandora and tucked the basket of bulbs under her arm so she could use her other hand to help her talk. Pandora would notice the movement and look up. Sometimes Rika's speech was a little shorn, even broken. "You look sad." Pandora smirked and shook his head.

"Sad? No, no! A little tired, to be honest. I guess I'm also a little worried about Mara. She seems angry at me." Rika tilted her head when Pandora looked down while talking. It was hard to read his lips when he did that. Pouting, Rika would think. Was he sad that Mara was being temperamental? It put her on edge too. That's what happened when you dealt with predators.

"Didn't you know?" She motioned her hand to her head. "She is a predator. They have been eating people because their food is drying up. She is probably hungry for birds or salamanders!" She warned, flailing a bit at the end of her thought. At this Pandora made a confused expression. He didn't think Mara was trying to kill him and... he heard rumors of the bandits and hunting parties sometimes feeding on their captured, but that was just rumors.

"Mara's not a bad person... she's just a little shy." Pandora muttered as he hurried into the kitchen to set the vegetables aside. Rika wasn't so sure, but let it go for now and delivered the basket of bulbs with Pandora. Mara had been standing to the side and heard them muttering about her as they entered. She quickly turned out the entrance and left.

"Mara --?!" Pandora turned around, thinking he saw her, but there was no one there. "Haa... I feel a little tired." He looked over to Rika. "If the Cardinal asks, I went to lay down. After all that jumping around the dump my legs are a little sore." Except he felt a lot of the weight on his shoulders. Rika would nod and motion her hand, sending him off with a wave.

Pandora made his way to the sleeping quarters so he could nap for a short while. Pushing open the door he would spot movement in the corner of his eye, on his cot. His feathers bristled as the fear struck him. Was someone messing with his pack?! But upon focusing he would see Mara laying on her stomach on his cot.

"Oh! Mara, hey." Pan closed the door behind him and walked over. Was she not mad at him like he thought? If she was tired too it would explain her strange behavior. Mara had her head laid in her arms and looked back at Pan whose tail feathers were spread open, twitching this way and that. She was laid out still in the church's garbs which consisted of a long red skirt and white, long sleeved tunic. She had replaced the one she had before as the sleeves had been torn. It didn't have a natural hole for her tail as it was expected members of the church hide even that part of themselves.

The tip of her tail would wiggle a bit at the skirt's hem before the appendage moved to curl up, pulling the fabric with it and putting on display the back of her leg's scales. The small speckles of orange scales stood out against her larger cerulean ones. It was then Pandora would see that between her thighs she had paler blue scales that didn't look like the other thick arrowhead shaped, natural armor. For just a moment he wondered if it was softer to the touch.

"Hey Mara?" He would finally blink. Mara murmured in a wordless response. She wasn't mad, right? The male moved to sit down beside her before he laid back with his head against the pillow. Mara moved closer to his body and would rest her leg against his side. Pandora would yawn and start to close his eyes. "Was worried you were mad at me..." She would shake her head at his words before glancing away. She was a little...

Before long the bird would fall asleep under the trappings of the predator's watch.

# CHAPTER EIGHT

## The Furry Arm Of The Law

Pandora felt rested after the nap. Though he was a little unsettled when he woke up with her arm around his neck and clawed hand by his face. It was a little startling, but seeing her relaxed face up close was kind of a treat. The entire time they were together she never seemed to let down her guard. The two would start getting up. Mara stretched her body out by pushing her arms forward, but since she was still laying on top of Pandora this ended up pushing her chest against his as her left arm pushed into his left cheek while her left cheek pushed into his right. He felt her jaws part and her hot breath roll against his ear. Her fingers stretched out, claws digging against the soft pillows as she stretched her muscles from her fingers to her toes and even the tip of her tail! The woman felt heavy on his chest because her muscles were dense. Unlike his which were springy and tightly wound. When the Drakus finally peeled herself off his body she would sit back and rub her eyes.

Pandora would be free to sit up. He stretched out his legs, letting his muscles tighten then relax. Those grasping claws of his flexed and were probably the most dangerous looking part of the bird, but Mara knew from first hand experience it was his legs. She watched as he stretched out his wings, one at a time, from shoulder to wing tip. She was amazed how long his feathers were and well kept. None of them seemed to be broken or missing meaning his molting seasons were well managed. She wanted to touch his wings and see just how they felt under her hands. The woman blinked when she noticed Pandora looking at her. After spreading out his tail feathers and stretching the last tight feeling out from his lower back, he would fold the wedge-shaped tail and turn to face the woman.

"Sorry I didn't believe you about..." He wanted to try and apologize and now that everything felt calmer he felt it was a good opportunity to talk to her. But as he tried to speak up Mara would move to stand and huff at him. She stomped forward and leaned her face close to his. He leaned his head back a bit, feeling her nose almost touching his.

"Don't -- it's fine.... it was my fault too. Just leave it." She snorted and moved to walk away. The Drakus hurriedly left the room, not letting him have a chance to talk back. The monk would smirk, chuckling softly as he watched her storm off. Before following the Drakus out the Avius moved to check the footlocker. He had a padlock and key that belonged to him and used it to seal up his pack. The key hung around his neck with his identification and he would pull it from his shirt before leaning in to unlock it. He opened it up to check on his bag and was satisfied to see it was still there. Being sure to lock everything back up the bird made his way out of the room to where Mara waited off to the side, her back leaned up against the wall. She stood up when she noticed Pandora, wanting to call out, but she resisted the urge rumbling in the back of her throat.

The pair walked over to one another and stood close. Pandora wasn't sure what to say to her now that things were peaceful. It was well into the early evening so good morning wasn't a viable choice. He suddenly felt his words wouldn't be enough. His still sleep-addled mind would start to catch up with his mouth, but as he was able to choke out her name, a commotion broke out in the main lobby of the church. The noise was enough to echo through the halls. Mara scoffed and turned her head away. Pandora sighed, but turned to make his way to the shrine. A number of the worshipers had been chased to the corners of the room while the priests stood in defense of the patrons. Cardinal Hash was standing in the center aisle facing off with warrant officer Greyfist and two of his men. Behind the rotund parish leader stood Rika, who was tucked behind his larger body with a fearful stance. Her small tail was tucked close to her body as she was ducked down. The owl Avius held his claws clutched together in front of his stomach and stood with his back straight.

"I'm pretty sure we talked about this Cardinal." Officer Greyfist stood before the Cardinal in uniform, which directly contrasted the red and white robes of the order with a forest green uniform with white accents. The opposing forces were regularly at odds with the law specifically denying heretics and their actions against societal law and how religion constantly tried to turn heretics over and lead them back into the world they had betrayed. The Artimmus faith made it even more difficult because they strongly prided themselves on their independence as a nation with the ability to work together towards a unified goal. "This is unacceptable!!" His roar carried so deep that the room shook with his echo. "All we ask of you Cardinal is to not house heretics! I've already heard questionable rumors concerning your order and here I come on a cordial visit to check on your little islander guest--!"

"What's going on...?" Though the sound of the Wolus' deep voice shook Pandora to his core he remained calm. Following up beside him was Mara who carried a proud stance. Her arms were crossed under her chest, pushing her breasts up enough to give her a powerful stance. "Maybe it's just because I'm from an island..." Pandora danced sarcastically over the officer's own words. "...but isn't this a time we should be having the evening meal and silent worship?" At Pandora's words some of the demi and kin parishioners looked up from behind the priests and would nod. They just wanted a peaceful night and not all this ruckus.

"Tch." The Wolus would scoff. "Well perhaps that's how it is in a tiny Oikos village, but this is a city. Artimmus faithfuls must always be ready to act and shine light on deception, such as with the Cardinal here. He said he wasn't hiding a heretic!" The warrant officer bore down on the Cardinal and reached out to grab him by the collar of his robes and began to growl down at him. Meanwhile the owl Avius flexed his talons as he was lifted up. One claw remained on the ground while the other began to lift up.

"Hey--!" Pandora stepped forward and reached out to grab Rika by her hand, pulling her to his side. Mara narrowed her eyes, but she would resist her urge to push Rika away and take her place. Instead the Drakus stood behind the Avius and glared at the Wolus from over his shoulder, backing up the little monk. The officer in question arched a brow. The other two officers reached for their batons, but the kin held out his paw, stopping them. "She's my follower!" The Wolus moved to release the Cardinal, who slowly placed both his feet back on the ground. When he was released he would puff up his wings before tucking them back at his sides, though he kept his claws curled and at the ready.

"What?" The Wolus spat out. "How many dangerous followers are you going to take in?! Aren't you even aware of yourself!?" The man would hold up his hand and stand over the bird, but kept his distance. With the bird's little Drakus he wasn't completely defenseless. He didn't want a conflict starting in the church where he could be held responsible. "If you keep picking up these degenerate heretics you'll end up with your bones stripped and thrown away in an alley!" Sadly the man's words had their validity, because there were many heretics that would sooner sell your hide to Slavers than help you.

"Well... even so," Pandora put his hands together. "I choose to trust them and that my good deeds help them see there are good paths to take." Though he was sure he could fend off a predator or two. That wasn't his only reason though. It was because it was also his duty to give everyone an equal opportunity. Everyone deserves a chance to show they could do good. "They've done nothing wrong." Pandora asserted. The warrant officer narrowed his eyes and lowered his head as his ears folded back in a threatening manner.

"I have my eye on you bird. One toe out of line and I will be sure to clap you and your followers in irons." He held up his hand before turning on his heel to leave, his two officers following him out. When the Wolus and his men left the priests worked to calm the parishioners and led them back to the pews. They would work to pray with them to help calm the situation. Meanwhile the Cardinal would turn to face Pandora. The man looked a little nervous, but was more so annoyed.

"You should have told me your other follower was a heretic..." The nervous owl moved to brush the end of his sash over his brow. "It brings trouble to the church. Even if you are a follower of Oikos and have your traditions, they just don't work here..."

"She's done nothing wrong, Cardinal. Rika isn't a heretic, just misunderstood. Please understand. She was just someone in need of help." Despite Pan's pleas the owl Avius looked at Rika and could see nothing but another heretic. Saurus and Drakus Tierans were all seen as heretics and were born and raised in heretic territory, but Salamandrus like Rika were often mistaken for them and accused of heresy with no more proof than a glance.

"Even still. There are rules ser Pandora. Please be mindful of them. You are here as a guest but you are still expected to be responsible. Consider this a favor..." The Cardinal would turn to leave, excusing himself from the stressful situation. Pandora sighed and felt his shoulders sink. The raven felt a little annoyed. The warrant officer only made his situation difficult. He didn't want to be seen as an ingrate nor as if he was not taking care to follow the rules. For a church the rules were as important as the doctrine was to the monastery. For now he could do nothing to make them understand. So long as Rika didn't have identification she would be seen as a heretic.

"Come on... let's finish helping and retire for the night." The monk exhaled. "We can get some more work done tomorrow. I want to earn as much as I can and do my work. The brothers of my order expect me to pass on the words of Oikos to others. Though if I can convince my own followers..." He looked over to Mara who scoffed and turned to walk off. He chuckled at her reaction. "I didn't think so.... what about you Rika?" The woman held up her hands, waving them in order to dismiss the man. She quickly covered her eyes so as to not see his words spoken and walked off after Mara. "....abandoned by my own flock!" He mused before moving to head to the kitchen so they could help with the evening meal.

# CHAPTER NINE

## A Criminal Act

Come the following morning Pandora was given his week's allowance by the church. Pandora was called into the Cardinal's office first thing that morning. Rika and Mara were sent to the kitchen to help with breakfast. Though Rika was a bit clumsy she showed herself to be quite efficient at peeling vegetables and Mara was surprisingly good at cooking. It surprised a few of the priests. Most of them just boiled the foods and served them with a bit of salt and pepper, but Mara used other spices and herbs they usually reserved for preserving meat. Most of the priests present were Wolus Tierans with a few Rodrus so they were usually somewhat tall or well figured demi and kin so seeing a Drakus as small as Mara was something of a treat. Though her height put her at odds with the others she didn't let it control the situation as she definitely acted much bigger than she was.

"W-what is this?" Pandora looked into the satchel, his tail twitching as his toes rapt against the ground. Inside the leather pouch appeared to be a stack of silver. The bird had never seen so much money in his life! There were at least five silver. What was going on? Was this some sort of trick? A ploy...? With this much he could buy a hundred, no! A thousand loaves of bread! "...with this much..."

"Yes, yes I know. It isn't much. You can hardly buy a decent seat at a restaurant, but trust me if you keep working hard there is plenty more coming. You see it is important to those of the Artimmus faith to be able to live independently and to do that one must be able to afford the necessities in life! I know you are probably used to the limited amenities of your monastery, but here you will have a little more than just a toothbrush and your sandals, although..." The owl Avius reached his claws up to his feathered chin as he leaned over slightly. He peered over his desk towards the tapping noise at the end of the table. "Well, perhaps you can afford some coverings for your feet too, hmm?" This suggestion caused Pandora to bristle. Why waste money on foot coverings when he's been fine without them! He'd be fine for longer.

"No, this is..." It was too much, were Pandora honest. But he could do with a little less upfrontness for now. "This is a start. But since I still have a way to go before I am independent..." He would never be independent. He grew up in Oikos. While he had a fundamental understanding of both religions there was no way he could accept not living with his brothers or having a system of support to fall back to when he was in a time of need. Those bonds he had built throughout his life weren't so easily broken. Oikos also aligned with his own, personal beliefs. He didn't feel people should be allowed to use their power to abuse others and knew that they deserved to be punished. Oikos only had three great rules he needed to remember and follow. "Did you have some things for me to do today? I want to try and help you guys out, an apology for getting you on the bad side of the officer." Though Pandora didn't feel he needed to apologize, the Cardinal would perhaps not turn his focus on Mara and Rika if he got him to let go of his caution towards his followers. The Cardinal would remove his bifocals from his beak and lower them so he could wipe the glass clean with his sash.

"Well, as a matter of fact I do. I think you can handle this since you worked at a Monastery. You are used to -- their type." Pandora wasn't sure what it was the Cardinal meant by that so he would listen to the man carefully. "Well we have some less fortunate that have gathered in one of our soup kitchens. While reaching out to the community is an important part of Artimmus, there is such a thing as working for oneself. It is important not to start depending heavily on others when you are capable of the work yourself. We need someone to gently lead the guests out of the kitchen and send them back into the world. While this is usually the job of our Bishops they have their hands full dealing with a more important task at my behest. Do you think you can do this?" What was Pandora even hearing?

"Y-yes. Sure." He shook the tremor out from his voice. "That seems easy enough." What did this man mean that he was used to this? Because of Oikos? They would never turn anyone away, nor would he demand that a person go off on their own without the necessary support. "If you'll excuse me." The owl Avius would smile and set his bifocals back over his beak. Pandora would leave the office feeling a little frustrated. How could this man ask him such things? Was he trying to get back at him because of Rika? It wasn't anyone's fault that Rika was in the situation that she was. Soon the Avius arrived at the dining hall where some of the priests were already on their way out to their tasks.

"If we hadn't taken our oaths already I wouldn't mind having that one as a wife, even if she doesn't have fur." One of the priests murmured underbreathe to his comrade as they left. Pan slowed to a stop at the comment. The raven allowed his eye to follow the men as they departed.

"Maybe..." The other began. "I don't think I could stand it. Those hard scales rubbing on my skin." He would shiver before both turned a corner. Pandora was a little relieved knowing those of the church were sworn to celibacy. For some reason the idea of them propositioning Mara or Rika rubbed him the wrong way.

While it wasn't his job to decide who they could talk to, the priests would hardly be his first choice if it was. Rika looked up from her empty bowl and reached out to tap Mara's shoulder. The Drakus clicked her tongue and glared at the salamander before the blonde woman pointed towards the entrance of the hall. When Mara caught Pan in her sights she stood.

"Pan!" At the sound of Mara's voice he was shaken from his dour contemplation. Turning his lips up into a smile he would walk over to the women. "Have you eaten yet? You always wake up way too early." She found that by the time she woke from her slumber he was already washed and ready to go for the day. When she stood from her spot she leaned forward, resting a hand on the table while the other picked up a bowl and handed it to him. "Here, we helped make the morning meal." She didn't let him squirrel away like he usually did and shoved it into his hands. Pandora frowned but would sip at the bowl. Mara waited expectantly. His eyes drifted up as he drank, feeling her gaze on him.

"Mmm," He raised his brows. "It's delicious." He didn't say such to appease her. He really thought as such. "Sorry if it's too early, but do you guys mind helping me clear the soup kitchen? Something the Cardinal asked me to do." The women tilted their heads. They looked at each other before looking back to Pandora. "Um, you don't usually find them in smaller villages. A soup kitchen is a place inside of the hospice where the poor are given a warm meal."

"The hospice?" Mara slowly spoke, as if trying to find the right words to use.

"Right. We were there yesterday, but we won't be doing anything except asking the people overstaying their welcome to leave." Pandora made sure he was clear enough for Mara that there were no ulterior reasons for them to go, not just yet anyway. It was just a task. Understanding the meaning behind his explanation the Drakus would nod, though she was a little less accepting of that than if they were going in order to stop that demented fiend.

Soon the three were making their way to the hospice, but the moment they left the church they would end up being followed. Warrant officer Greyfist had decided to stake out the church along with a Lawman from the district. Though officer and lawmen were sometimes used interchangeably they were very different organizations. The Officers were usually the naval military that existed within the docks to maintain order, while the lawmen enforced the law of the city on all fronts. If it came from the docks it was the responsibility of the officers, but if it was a problem within the city it fell to the lawmen. Though Greyfist was sure the Cardinal was up to something, it was his job to make sure the Oikos ardent kept within his allowable duties. While Artimmus faithfuls looked down on the Oikos faith it was a recognized religion as it was the oldest known practice on the planet, dating back as far as prehistory. Warrant officer Greyfist was determined to catch the Avius on the wrong side of the law so he could put him away once and for all.

"Why do we have to send them away...?" Rika rubbed her hand to her chest before splaying her hand out towards Pandora in question. When he better explained their task the Salamandrus found herself not seeing the sense in it. "If the hospice is for the poor to rest, why can they not stay?" While Pandora felt that it wasn't right these people had to be kicked out for little more than having nowhere else to go, he also felt it was better they acted for the church because of the deeper dangers of the place Mara and he were aware of.

"I don't like it either, but that's how Artimmus feels that it helps people. Though it isn't a case of Oikos versus Artimmus, we would never be allowed to do such a thing in Oikos." Pandora explained. "It's seen as doing willful harm. It is against the main laws of our religion to willfully do harm to others if it can be helped. Of course we are allowed to defend ourselves, our family, and our homes." He noted. With that in mind Pandora would sigh. Heading into the hospice he would approach the counter to talk to the nurse on duty. Sadly it wasn't the more familiar Miru, but they were quickly taken to the kitchen area of the hospice, nevertheless.

The kitchen was a large room with an open hearth that kept the area warm. There were a few long tables with stools for visitors to partake in the proffered meals and a small staff of volunteers working in the kitchen to prepare what would be today's lunch. The man they were supposed to be removing was a young Rodrus Tieran who had recently lost his home due to his gambling habits. The man was a demi and wore simple trousers with a blue, tattered, tunic and a black shirt underneath that helped to keep him warm and somewhat clean. Pandora motioned his hand to Mara and Rika.

"Let me talk to him..." He didn't want the girls to get their hands into this, at least not just yet. He didn't want them feeling guilty or blaming themselves were something to happen to the man. The Avius approached the Rodrus. His long, pink tail hung from his trousers and dragged along the floor. He sat with his hairless hands clasped together and sitting on the table while his knee bounced anxiously just beneath the surface. His eyes were glazed over with an exhausted look. His skin was pale, almost translucent from his malnutrition, having been struggling months on end to find a regular meal. "Hey...." Pandora moved to seat himself beside the Rodrus.

"Father, is that you?" The rat Rodrus spoke. "I know I haven't come home, but I've almost won." He chuckled, holding out his hand in order to rest it over Pan's, which lay on the table's surface. The man's hands were hot to the touch. In fact they almost burned Pandora with how warm he felt. The bird would flinch and look over to the rat. "Isn't it... lovely?" Suddenly he would begin to foam at the mouth, turning his gaze towards Pandora's. "Your eyes.... they look delicious... RAUGH!" The

Rodrus lunged at Pandora, but he was quick to scuttle back and shove the rat off the bench.

# CHAPTER TEN

## A Touch Too Far

The attack happened so fast that Pandora wasn't even able to think before pushing the man down and moving to pin him. He pressed his knee down onto the middle of his back, but the more he held him down the more he struggled. The rat Rodrus was strong, stronger than Pandora! After moments of struggling the rat was able to roll and slash Pandora across the face, sending him to the ground. The raving man screamed out nonsensical words.

"Get back! No more! I don't want to drink anymore!" The Rodrus howled as he shrieked and pulled his hands to the side of his face. At this point he had clenched down on his jaws so hard his mouth was bleeding. Whatever was happening it was causing him immense pain. Pandora tried to stand, but the Rodrus stomped his foot down on the man's back.

"Pan!" Mara was the first to act. Others around them had begun to panic. Some of the visitors hurried away with their precious few belongings while the volunteers ducked down behind their counters and tried to peer around the corner at the commotion. This wasn't the first time this had happened and it seemed that whenever it did someone was either hurt or died as a result.

Mara rushed the Rodrus and pushed her covered arm against his chest, forcing him off the raven. "Pan, are you okay?!" She reached out to grab him. Though in pain Pandora took her hand and pulled himself to his feet.

"Reeeauugh!!" The sound of the Rodrus roaring alerted Pandora and he moved to pull his wings around Mara as he pulled the Drakus against his chest. Rika had already hidden away from the chaos, the crazed man still rampaging. The raven Avius winced in pain when he felt the man slash his claws across the middle of his back, right against his shoulder blades.

"There!" A deep voice called from the entrance of the kitchen. Two large Orderlies ran towards the rat and would tackle him to the ground. The Rodrus viciously fought against being subdued and bit his attackers who responded by beating him down with their batons. Another Orderly soon entered, followed by a nurse. This Orderly was a large Ursus and he moved to kneel down behind the snarling man as the other two pinned his legs and knees. The Ursus dropped his large hand against the top of the Rodrus head to hold him still. The nurse stepped in to inject him with some medicine. It looked to take effect almost instantly as the Rodrus began to relax. "Tie him up. We're taking this one to the hospital like the rest." The Ursus ordered. Pandora couldn't believe what he was seeing. Was this the 'hysteria' affecting the patrons of this hospice?

Soon after Pan was checked over by the nurses for his injuries. He didn't accept any medicine, knowing it wouldn't do him any good anyway. Afterwards Pandora, Mara, and Rika would leave the hospice. They were silent on the way back to the church. Mara walked beside Pandora who held his right hand over his left arm. Being slammed by the Rodrus had hurt more than he expected. Rika followed behind the two, a bit despondent that she had been unable to garner the courage to help Pandora like Mara had. Mara was uncentered by the whole ordeal. While it was frightening to see someone lose their senses in such a way it had been more startling that Pan was overcome. She viewed Pandora as a strong person, but that Rodrus had thrown him aside so easily. Yet despite this she felt herself further drawn to his side rather than pushed away by his defeat.

"A-are you..." Mara cursed the uncertainty in her voice. "Are you okay? Why did you throw yourself at me like that? My scales would have --" Pan glanced over towards Mara, his brows furrowing in annoyance. She found her words becoming stuck in her throat. When she lost her will to scold Pan the Avius smiled, though it was the kind of smile a person used to hide their inner thoughts from others.

"I'm glad you're alright Mara." Pandora would offer, only for the Drakus to nod. "I'm fine. I was the responsible party." Yet he was unable to do anything to help that man. Not only was he about to throw him out on the street with no food, but in such a state. Had he succeeded in removing him from the facility someone out here could have been seriously hurt and it would have been his fault. This was what he deserved, at the very least. It was his Karma for trying to bring harm to someone, however indirect it seemed. "You are... alright, right?" He slowed to a stop before turning to face the Drakus. She felt her scales tighten suddenly as she stiffened and found herself wanting to back away, but it was too late. She felt Pandora's hand press against the small of her back, pulling her close as he seemed to inspect her.

"Yes!" She barked. "Let's go back and rest!" She felt Pandora was acting strange and needed it. "Oy!" She let out a surprised sounding shout when she felt his hand brush down over the top of the base of her tail which he would pet and turn to leave. Mara shivered before she snapped her gaze over at Rika who quickly looked away, her face blushing. For those like Drakus, Saurus, and even Salamandrus the tail was sensitive near the base for many reasons.

Pandora reported the situation to the Cardinal.

"I see, well it must have been difficult. That is alright." Cardinal Hash soothed. "More and more seem to be getting sick every day, but that is the problem when one starts losing their faith. Come, I'll consider this task complete even if its outcome was quite different than expected! Let's keep you three busy. Would you mind handling the laundry? We have accumulated quite a bit!" With that resolved Pandora and the girls set off on their next task.

They would have to collect laundry from the sleeping quarters, the bathing rooms, and kitchens in order to take them to be scrubbed by hand, spun by machine, before being hung to dry. Rika worked on collecting the loads from the different rooms in order to bring them outside to the churchyard where a small canal ran through which they used to wash their linens. Mara worked to scrub the cloth while Pandora loaded what she finished scrubbing into a machine that spun the laundry through use of a manual device he cranked a handle to turn before he hung them to dry. He moved to crouch down beside Mara while he waited for the next load to spin.

"You could help scrub, you know!?" She snapped her fangs in his direction only for the bird to sit down and dip his legs in the canal. She sighed and continued to work, ignoring Pandora. While she focused on scrubbing she would feel a hand brush along her knee. Mara was crouched over the water and used a bar of soap with a scrubbing board to force suds through the cloth in order to wash away the dirt. When she looked over to her leg she'd find Pan's hand on her scaled limb. "What are you...?"

"I'm sorry." Pan spoke up in a quiet tone. "I almost let you get hurt...." He continued to rub her knee and before moving down the side towards her hip. Mara found herself moving to sit down on the edge of the canal. She either wanted him to stop so had sat, or she wanted him to continue and had sat. The Drakus and Avius weren't sure which situation they were facing. "Do you want I stop?" He would ask. Mara thought for a moment and shook her head. Maybe she did want him to stop, just not yet. A soft sound bubbled up from behind them, catching their attention. Rika cleared her throat, having brought more cloth for the wash. Pan sucked on his tooth and rolled to stand to his feet and return to spinning.

But that would not be the last incident.

The next time, Mara would approach Pan, soliciting him for his attention. At this moment they found themselves handling the garden duties. Digging up the vegetables the church cultivated to use in the kitchen, Pandora was using his talons to dig up the tubers that grew under the soil. Mara leaned herself close to the raven Avius and hiked up the fabric of her skirt slightly in order to expose her scaled legs. She was carrying a basket to collect the vegetables he dug up, but now used her current role to get in close to the man. She rubbed her scaled thigh against his softer, feather covered one. Instead of discouraging her, Pandora reached out his wing to lean against her back so she could raise her leg higher.

"Hey, Mara, is your home very far from here?" Pan would wonder. Mara nodded her head, feeling her chance to arch her leg higher. He hummed in thought. "Maybe we can go see it after my pilgrimage..."

"I don't know..." She shook her head. "It's full of rotten and ornery Drakus that wouldn't give up the chance to try and snatch you up..." She looked up towards his face and parted her jaws. She just wanted to nibble his neck a bit. But before she could submit to her desire, Rika once again cleared her throat upon catching them in the act. She had a second basket full of vegetables and the two barely had completed their first. The bird snorted and hopped to his left, moving away from Mara before he returned to digging. The Drakus turned her eyes towards the Salamandrus who stared at her in exacerbation.

Warrant officer Greyfist stood in the Cardinal's office, his fists on his hips as they watched through the window which usually had its curtain drawn during the day. "You need to teach that miscreant a lesson, Cardinal, or it'll put the whole church's reputation on the line... It's already thinning with these questionable rumors about your use of funds." The Wolus growled in amusement. If he had to play a little dirty to get that bird straightened out, so he will.

-

-

-

Pandora and Mara were called into the Cardinal's office sometime later. By the end of the day, interruptions aside, they managed to complete all of their tasks, but it seems Rika had not been the only one catching them in the act. The owl Avius sighed, moving his claws to lift his sash in order to brush the side of his head, the stress feeding the nervous tick. Pandora had taken the seat, but Mara would stand by the door with her arms crossed over her chest. She made her displeasure clear.

"Pandora, I've noticed some problematic things today." Cardinal Hash tried to remain polite, though the young Avius was definitely stretching his charity to the limit. "You have been witnessed taking advantage of your relationship with your Drakus follower." He glanced up at Mara before looking back to Pandora who was seated and calmly listening. Pandora wasn't sure what to say in response to the accusation. He certainly wasn't taking advantage of Mara. He wasn't sure if that was possible given her personality. "Well -- I feel you're having a difficult time adjusting to our ways. While I fully understand as a member of Oikos you are lacking in many ways, but I think I have an idea that will help not only you, but your two -- followers." In the end they were heretics and it would look better for the church if they were properly trained.

"What do you have in mind?" Pandora wasn't sure what had the owl on edge. The man seemed to always have a difficult time with his temperament and patience.

"Ah, hoho!" He chuckled. "Well I was thinking of sending you and your followers to some traditional training we send Artimmus priests to before they graduate to act upon their daily tasks and the expectations held here at the church. Now I don't want to seem as if I'm pushing our faith on you. You have your ways, but it would look good if you perhaps keep an open heart and participate. Perhaps you can learn something new that will help you expand your limited skillsets." Pandora knew it was true that there was much he didn't know. He was still young and had only just left the village. Being that he was on his pilgrimage it was his duty to learn as much of the world as he could and that also meant understanding the other faiths that existed on Tier. Aside from Oikos and Artimmus there were many other types of worship that had developed over its growth as a society. "Please... you see the Cleric will be coming to the church soon and I want to make sure everyone acts appropriately in her presence." Pandora, though reluctant, did want to try and learn more about the Artimmus faith and why it was so -- selfish seeming. Maybe it was his lack of understanding. He was there as a guest and it would behoove him to accept his host's offer for an expanded education.

"Of course, where is this training?" At Pandora's agreement the Cardinal would let out a deep sigh.

"Oh hoho, well it is a place we of the Artimmus faith work as a means to learn humility, responsibility, and self-sufficiency. It is a large ranch just outside the city called Red Geode Ranch. Quite so because it is known for its red rock outcroppings as it sits along Red Ridge." The Cardinal explained. "I will sign you and your followers up as we are sending one of our younger priests and it would help him immensely having some company." With that Cardinal Hash would sign Pandora, Mara, and Rika up for a month of work at Red Geode Ranch.

# CHAPTER ELEVEN

## Seasonal Preparations

Pandora waited while the Cardinal worked to sign the necessary documents for him to participate in the Ranch. The raven Avius balked at the sight of all the pages of words that detailed the lessons and activities to participate in while there. Because Pandora was unable to read he would ask the Cardinal directly.

"So what exactly would we be learning? How was your experience?" He'd ask the man of his personal time spent at the camp lest he be told to just look over the literature. "Surely you must have excelled!" The Cardinal set down his pen and looked over to Pandora, a smile pulling up the corners of his beak.

"While I would like to say I was a brilliant pupil, I cannot say I was. It was quite difficult for me. My seniors were incredibly tough and being weak willed as I was in my youth I was always on the verge of tears! It was difficult for me to understand at the time, but they were there to help me and make sure that I succeeded. Being a follower of Artimmus is difficult because we have to support ourselves and stand on our own power, but in the end it means that, like Artimus herself, we will shine brightly even during the day for the sacrifices we make!" He sighed and nodded. "You will come out a stronger person, don't you worry!" But Pandora couldn't help but worry that he wasn't ready for this. So far the Artimmus faithfuls have shown a distinct reliance on things like money or material goods. While he could admit he liked things, he's lived so long with so little he wasn't sure what to do with everything the church was providing him. But that brought on a thought.

"Will I need anything while at the Ranch?" If they were going to be learning independence would he need to know how to read or even bring matches? He wouldn't be able to start a fire if he needed to!

"Ah yes. While the Ranch will provide housing, work clothing, and clean water it is you that must provide your own food, bring your own toiletries. So I would highly suggest you bring your money with you!" Cardinal Hash would tidy up the papers before he moved to look over each leaflet before he grunted in satisfaction. "There, all done. Here you are. Just make sure to hold onto this. This will be your identification to be allowed into the Ranch." He stood and handed Pandora the paperwork. The raven Avius looked down to the sheets, acting as if he was going through it in detail.

"Great. Well if I have to prepare for this venture I'll need to get some supplies." But he wasn't sure what he would need, but he was sure where he wanted to go. He had some things to ask about as well.

"Feel free to use tomorrow to do so! Despite your -- " The Cardinal cleared his throat. "...problematic distractions, you were able to get all your tasks done. I will pay you appropriately and you can head off tomorrow to get what you will need. Be sure to think carefully ser Pandora. The Ranch tests a man's fortitude and a woman's resilience. So be sure to take your two followers. They will benefit from it!"

The next morning Pandora decided to head to the Eye of Newt. He wanted to ask about this ranch from a person who seemed to have more worldly experience and get a few supplies that he felt would be more pertinent at a farm environment. It wasn't uncommon to get injuries at places like this and sickness was often rampant. After all, clinics were more commonplace in towns with farms or built near them. He heard it was common to be bitten by the animals there and the tools were usually irregularly maintained that also led to injury. Though Pan was willing to go alone Mara insisted she come and Rika was curious about this place. Making their way to the docks they soon found themselves passing the Pearlescence. Unlike that day the front gates had been closed and sealed with metal chains. Even the warehouse doors and factory doors looked to be sealed up.

"Oh, if it isn't Pandora and Mara!" Jasper's voice called from the distance as they neared the property. The Ursus was in his usual coveralls. Working with medicines and potions was hazardous so the coveralls were a good way to avoid being splashed or having your fur and skin permanently stained by the various concoctions that were handled. "I hope you got to the church safe and sound?" The man was worried since they left. The strange lad wandering around with a heretic was something of special interest to the officers of the docks because foreigners were usually looked at with great suspicion because they often brought with them ill intentions.

"Hello again!" Pandora greeted, finding the good nature of the Ursus refreshing after having spent just two days at the Artimmus church. "I was able to, yes. Thank you again for everything." Pandora did not want to sound ungrateful and unload his complaints onto the Ursus, so he decided to just keep his complaints to himself. "Though there was something I wanted to ask." Jasper perked up, his attention on the young bird. "Have you heard of a place called Red Geode Ranch?" After his question was voiced there was an awkward space left in the air that didn't fill the raven with confidence.

"Well, uh..." The Ursus rubbed the back of his head with his large hand. "Red Geode, huh? Well heard of the place for sure. Never been there though. Why would you be going to such a place though?"

"Haha..." Pandora dryly laughed. "Well the church asked me to go so I can learn a bit more about their rules and such." The Ursus grunted in understanding. So that was how it was, huh? He knew that Oikos and Artimmus had their differences, but to think.

"Well, I don't want to assume, since it's usually a place priestly sorts go...--" Jasper wasn't the sort to gossip and the rumors were, frankly, unfounded so it didn't seem fair to tell the tale!

"The place is creepy!" A familiar voice rang through the air. Pandora looked over and stepping up beside Jasper was a healthy looking young kin Ursus with bright eyes and blushing cheeks. "Hello ser monk! It's so good to see you again, and healthy and hale!" She put her paws together and bowed her head to the monk. Clinging to her skirt appeared to be a young Ursus wearing a white smock and galoshes. Pandora blinked in surprise before he stood up a bit on his feet.

"Mayweather? You look so different!" She looked amazing! By the looks of it she had gained some weight and filled out her skirt. She wore a loose blouse with an apron over the outfit. "Wait, is--" He pointed to Jasper. Mayweather crossed her paws in front of her and nodded.

"Oh yes, this is the uncle I was telling you about. Harvy and I settled in well. I sometimes help my auntie at the Bunkhouse with cleaning." She spoke with a cheerful demeanor, no different than the gentle woman he had met on the boat, just much healthier with a fair deal of weight more natural looking on an Ursus' frame. Mara pushed up close to Pan and glared in the brown Ursus' direction.

"Who's this?" Mara looked the woman up and down. She was a big girl and looked like she could take off a head or two with those arms. She was tall, making her wonder if Pan had a thing for tall girls. Mayweather didn't seem to have much in the way of chest so she was safe there. Pandora rolled his eyes and looked towards Mara.

"This is Mayweather. She was on the ship coming this way with her baby brother." He would point to the cub who stood holding onto the woman, his paw shoved into his muzzle. Mara's tail shuffled against the ground before she glanced away. With that Mara thought better than to pry too much lest oust herself as the bandit on the boat. "Now what did you mean by creepy?" He would ask, turning his attention to Mayweather. The Ursus woman looked to her uncle, who chuckled nervously.

"Well, my uncle is a little too nice about it, but some of the people that weren't able to become priests would talk about how strange things happened there and it had made it difficult for them to even sleep on the island. They struggled quite a bit because between the hard work and strange encounters they would get no sleep and the challenges led by senior members were almost impossible, but that isn't the creepy part." Mayweather put her finger to her muzzle. "I heard from a number of the female attendants that they would be watched when in private. And many of the males engaged in rutting competitions."

"Excuse me...?" Pandora looked to Jasper who coughed into his fist. "Island? Rutting competitions?" Rika turned her head away as Mara moved to cross her arms over her chest, a look of disgust on her face.

"I've had to deal with that before..." Mara would admit. "Males get into competing with one another to get the attention of a woman to mate with. But when done outside of nesting season it's seen as immature. Gross." Certain groups would have children during specific seasons in order to make sure their villages and towns had enough food and supplies to support the population boom. Cities didn't have to worry about nesting seasons as much and women tended to be in estrus more regularly as opposed to the irregular times with more resource conscious groups. To Pandora it sounded -- strange. It wasn't as if he wasn't aware of the idea, but actually seeing it was something he never experienced. "They can get dangerous though because they end up taking stupid risks or sometimes harassing the female until she..." She let her words hang, unwilling to face the disastrous situation that sometimes ended up happening. Mayweather nodded.

"Yes. Ursus are normally from places with heavy snowfall so our nesting seasons begin in the start of spring so that we give birth by the start of the colder seasons and keep the cubs safe with us during hibernation." It was the most efficient way Ursus learned to have young as the southern mainland became barren during the dry season, which was also their cold season. Many mothers have been known to starve because families were unable to reach the nest sites that hadn't thawed.

"Aren't priests supposed to be celibate?" Pandora questioned. It seemed a bit troublesome, but that is something that shouldn't happen to begin with. Pandora didn't think a person should withhold themselves from their desires, but there were ways to express them that were safe and didn't oppress. Self-imposed celibacy seemed oppressive.

"No." Jasper spoke up. "They don't take those vows until they return from that training, if they choose to complete their training. But you shouldn't worry about it. I mean you're partners, aren't you?" Mara was always so close with Pandora that he had assumed they were already mated. As far as he knew monks didn't make any vows involving taking mates. He knew an old monk from when he was younger that had grandchildren!

"What?!" Mara barked, sputtering a bit before she stamped her foot. It wasn't even close to the cold season, which was the normal time of year for Drakus to start making nests. That wasn't the point though. "Why would you think that?!" At her reaction Rika would giggle. Pandora was a little wounded, but it passed.

"No, we aren't. She's my follower and because of that I'll make sure to take care of her, and Rika." He glanced back at the salamander who hid herself behind some boxes to stay out of view. Chuckling softly Pandora turned his attention back to Jasper and Mayweather. "Well, I don't want to waste your time, but do you think you can get me some things I may need at the Ranch...?"

# CHAPTER TWELVE

## Baptism

The whole conversation had baffled Pandora. He had never seen rutting competitions that were intended to get a woman's attention, or a partner of any kind. This was probably because in his village all of the members belonged to the commune and it was the women who were in charge of keeping nests in order, even when it was time to start preparing. It sounded like an annoying event. He wasn't one for showing off nor did he get any sort of pleasure trying to expend the energy to make himself look good in front of somebody else. If it was left up to Pandora he would be the one hibernating. But he was still thankful for the effort they put into explaining it to him. He didn't want to be caught in the open and be accused of misunderstanding someone. He wondered if Drakus or Salamandrus did such things, though if what Mara said had validity to it males had tried so with her. She didn't sound very impressed and that made him feel immensely satisfied.

"So what kinda stuff are you looking for?" Jasper had brought the three into the warehouse where their shelves were stocked full of all kinds of medicines one could ever need. "I know you'll be on Red Ridge so you'd definitely want to protect against Ague and Breakbone Fever." The black Ursus moved around the shelves with a small stack of paper he had gotten from Pandora.

It was the activities they would be partaking in while on the island. But that was what stood out the most to Pan. It wasn't the degenerate concept of boasting to earn oneself a chance at being in the arms of another, but the island part.

"Why is the ranch on an island?!" How did they get livestock back and forth? Could they even grow usable plants on that island? The problem with many islands on Tier was that they were too rocky to grow anything viable.

"That's on account of its seclusion." Jasper explained. "It lets people rough it far from the city, but you don't have to worry too much since you're from a village. It's the diseases they have over there that you and your lot may not be used to. So it's good to take something before you go, also some medicine for the evening. You might get sick from the sudden change in environment." Pandora gave Jasper a confused look. "Ah, it rains quite a lot on the island even during the winter. In spring it's a near constant storm so you'll definitely need something for Camp Fever." He picked out a bottle that seemed full of a hazy looking liquid. "What else were you looking for?" He looked over to Pandora who was staring up at the bottles, unable to read anything. He would recall something Mara had mentioned about her healer.

"Do you have medicine for Gripe?" He looked over to Jasper. Mara had mentioned her hunters get medicines from the healer before leaving as preventative measures so they didn't catch the disease and bring it back home. Mara was off to the side listening to the workmen talk. They had become fond of the Drakus because she listened to them and showed interest in their ideas or concoctions that few customers did. Most just wanted the right medicine and didn't care how it worked. Mara definitely endeared herself to the apothecaries. Mara tilted her head slightly as she turned her gaze over to Pandora. As for Rika she walked around with Mayweather who was now carrying Harvy in her arms.

"As you see they take care not to store these bottles in the light. It can change the effect of the medicine you know." Mayweather patiently explained to Rika, who watched her intently. "I know it isn't the most riveting sounding thing, but the side effects that result can be quite chaotic to handle after the fact. Some medicines cause convulsions or cause people to break out in hives!" She looked to Rika who tilted her head. "I'm sorry. Was I blabbing...?" She would worry. Rika shook her head and held up her hand, moving her fingers as she spoke.

"Actually, do you have medicine that can fix damaged body parts?" She would move her hands to herself as she expressed her thoughts. "Like if the voice didn't work anymore, or the ears?" Mayweather would tap her chin in thought. It would be nice if there were more types of medicines, but of all the ones she knew that wasn't one.

"I don't know very much about the medicines available in other places so there could be something like that, but there aren't any here that I've heard of. But I'm sure there's medicine like that somewhere." She looked at Rika and nodded. "I heard that there are so many kinds of medicines that can cure somebody completely of any disease!" It was amazing to think about it. "But here well... it's all great medicine even if it can't do that. I'm sorry." She felt as if she was talking far too much. "Why are you looking for something like that? Is someone you know severely injured?" Rika smiled, shaking her head.

"No, no," She motioned her hand to the negative as she shook her head. "I was just curious, thank you. You are knowledgeable about medicine." After looking around a bit with Mayweather the two would return to one of the work tables where Pandora, Mara, Jasper, and a few apothecaries were talking. Pandora looked up, Mara glancing back when the Avius turned his head away from her. She was standing close to him, showing off the bottle of medicine that the workers made especially for her. The Drakus curled her lip at Pandora and would growl. The Avius reached up to pet the side of Mara's face in order to appease her before he stepped back from the table.

"Oh, Mayweather, Rika. Did you find what you were looking for?" He would ask the salamander. The woman would lower her head, shaking it to the negative. "Ah -- I see." He would frown. Rika moved off to the side as Mayweather approached, still carrying Harvy on her hip. Rika had said she wanted to see if they had had certain medicine that was difficult to find. She hadn't told him what exactly it was, but it was probably none of his business. "I think that was everything on our list. Though, since you're here -- Mayweather I wanted to ask you something." Mara narrowed her eyes at Pandora before turning around to face the Ursus who pulled her muzzle up in a smile. "You had asked me for help on the ship, does that mean your Oikos instead of Artimmus?" Ursus were from the southern regions and they were primarily Artimmus faithfuls.

"Oh! Yes, yes!" She clapped her paws together, adjusting Harvy on her hip. "I had a difficult time after my mother died and couldn't find anyone to help me through that difficult time. But there's a monk that lives there, walked with me through my grief. It helped me immensely, and he helped Harvy too. Harvy here was baptized." She giggled, taking Harvy's free paw onto hers and danced with him. Mara stood back and looked over to Pandora who seemed a bit surprised by her words.

"What does baptizing do, anyway?" The Drakus questioned. She watched as Pan's expression changed before he shook his head and smiled that smile again. He had mentioned that Oikos faithful got baptized, but Mayweather had only mentioned the cub participating in the tradition and not herself. Mayweather seemed to be focused on the cub and Mara didn't want to ask her because she wanted to hear it from the monk. From Pandora. He looked at Mara and motioned his hand. He didn't expect to be put on the spot and felt it wasn't the type of topic to discuss in public.

"I'll tell you later. They're kind of private events." He'd regard her. "But we should be getting back. Thanks so much for your help Jasper!" Pan turned away from Mara, trying not to look her in the eye. Though the Drakus knew something was strange with his avoiding the topic, she knew she couldn't just force it out of him, especially with how much of a stink she made about not getting baptized by him to become a follower. Jasper smiled and handed Pandora the papers back.

"I read some of it and it looks pretty ordinary. Just watch out for yourselves because being independent is held above all else by the Artimmus faithful. Artimus gives us trials that sometimes bring us suffering, so even if you were struggling desperately you may not find anyone willing to lend a helping paw." He warned. Making sure they had everything packed up, the three would return to the church.

# CHAPTER THIRTEEN

## Kokivorosdos Island

After returning from the Eye of Newt the three continued to do tasks for the church. Mara was particularly stressed by the attention Mayweather had been given by Pandora. The Ursus woman was strong looking. She had muscles that the Drakus couldn't even account for. The female was also far outside her weight class and could easily become a knight had she desired. The cub only added to her charm making her seem to be a good caretaker and mother, something Mara never saw herself doing. She was too strict in her ways and didn't feel being gentle made for a good parent. Her mother was gentle and she felt she turned out awful. She spent much of their day putting on displays for the bird. She tried to draw his eye by occasionally putting her leg on display or feats of strength by carrying more than usual, but nothing seemed to catch his eye. Rika on the other hand was having quite an easy time getting his attention. The weak and clumsy little salamander was able to get his help, or called out to him when she couldn't understand how to do a task. Did he like helpless girls? Mara wasn't helpless though...

"Mara, are you listening?" Mara blinked and turned her attention to Pandora. It was the next day and he was packing up his knapsack with a few other supplies, the ones they had gotten from the Eye of Newt. She was sitting on his cot, her tail splayed out and hanging over the edge. She had been moping, softly growling as she watched him pack. He wasn't sure what had her so grumpy, but he would leave her to her shifting moods. "You seem out of it. Are you sure you want to come after hearing all that from Mayweather?" He reached out to touch the side of her leg, which was exposed with how she laid. Mara was on her side, legs crossed in a way that had tugged up her skirt in the process of moving around as she tried brushing her scales against his bedding in order to subtly rub her scent into his space.

"I'm fine..." Mara watched his hand as it rubbed into her scales and slowly moved up her leg. Pandora still found himself curious about that soft looking coat of scales near her inner thigh, but he put it aside for now and let his hand slide away. He pulled the strings of his pack taut and nodded to the woman. "I still don't see why you have to go. It seems arrogant of him to think he can change you." Pandora rubbed the side of his head at her words. Had she noticed?

"Well we don't want to be kicked out and it shouldn't be terrible." A month was a long time though. "It'll give me a chance to meditate anyway. The church doesn't really give their members much time to themselves to do anything outside of their duties." Mara moved to sit up, tilting her head at the bird. "Well a person should have time to themselves to decompress and the way we do that in the monastery is to meditate. So I'll take advantage of that." He looked back to the bed where Rika was sitting. The horns on top of her head had been twitching, but she didn't seem to be participating in their chatter, or even listening. He was about to turn around and call out to Rika. Noticing this Mara quickly moved to stand on her knees and throw her arms over Pandora's shoulders, her chest pressing against his as she kept him from turning. They were face to face and she would narrow her eyes into an annoyed glare.

"*I'm right here.*" She whispered. "*Why do you need to pay attention to her?*" Pandora found himself blinking in confusion, his mind a little boggled by the woman's behavior. What did she want him to say? There was no deeper reasoning behind his actions. It was a simple act of courtesy. Right?

"Should I just ignore her?" he asked a question to answer hers. At this Mara would peek over his shoulder at Rika who looked at Mara with a deep sense of confusion painted on her features. "You should be nicer to her. Once we get her some proper identification we can get back to dealing with the hospital. This is a step towards them trusting us." Mara considered his words a moment before she spoke up.

"Fine. But won't it just get worse if we spend time playing around on some island?" Her question was valid, but it was already pretty bad.

"Well we asked Jasper to help, right? He should have some information for us, but it'll take time to gather it. We don't know anything about the person in charge of the hospice or who that doctor was... they could be important people which would make it harder for us to deal with." He explained in a low tone that hung just between them. Mara would slide back and sit on the back of her legs. "Good girl." he chuckled, reaching over to pet the side of her face.

Not long after packing their things, they would be led by the Cardinal to the port. Mara had been given a pack to store away a few clothes and her medicine bottles. Pandora was given another fifteen silver, putting him at twenty for their trip. The boat that would be carrying the faithful off towards the island was docked just off the wharf where they were gathered. The captain of the ship was an old Wolus kin with grey fur. He wore a heavy, salt crusted coat and had a peg leg. Atop his head, held between his thick, triangular ears was a tattered old cap that kept his skull warm on the cold oceanic currents. He was looking down at a clipboard and would check off the names of the ardents as they boarded one by one. Pandora looked over to

Cardinal Hash. They had come with them and the young priest-in-training that would be going with them. His name was Ash and he was around Pandora's age. The Cardinal had wanted Pandora to just keep the fellow company as he was shy.

"Now, now Ash I know you have what it takes." The Cardinal fussed over the boy and it was now obvious as to why. Ash was his nephew.

"Of course, uncle..." He was a tall, lanky Avius kin with a codified look expected of young priests. He had loose robes that covered him from head to toe. They were red robes that he wore with white trousers beneath and white foot coverings. Even his wings were draped in white silks that were decorated with silver chains. Over his beak hung a pair of glasses with a silver chain that held it over his feathered earholes that occasionally twitched with passing sounds. "D-don't worry. Ser Pan will be keeping me company.... right?" He looked over to Pan and held out his clawed hands.

"No, please.... call me Pandora." He reached out his hand to take Ash's and rested his palm to the man's. "We're both going there to better ourselves, right?" He would look over to Cardinal Hash, understanding well why the man put him under his care after hearing of things from both the owl's experience and Mayweather's gossip. He wanted to ensure his nephew had support... Soon it was their turn to sign in. Pandora walked up to the Wolus Captain. He held out the papers that the Cardinal had prepared for him and Mara.

"What are ya showin' me!?" The Wolus bit out, with a playful grin. "Get on board. Don't care none if yer here to pray or here ta stowaway. Just be sure you work and don't touch my loads!" They could see just behind them the cranes lowering cargo onto the captain's sturdy vessel. Pandora nodded and moved his hand to the small of Mara's back before leading the woman up onto the vessel. Ash followed behind and made sure not to meet the old captain in the eyes before he followed along. "Damn kids." It wasn't as if he didn't know why he was here. Sure the paperwork was needed to prove what they were going to the island for.

Passage to the island was strictly controlled as it was the only place red quartz geodes could be mined. The geodes were vital for Mene's steel manufacturing industry as it was used to cast the metal sheets in order to shape them into the various forms used throughout construction. It was also vital in the manufacture of Crystals. The only means to grow Crystals outside of the natural habitats in which they grew was using quartz as a base in order to process the high quality stones used in jewelry, watchmaking, and some small electric devices that were still in the testing phases of production in some areas of Mene.

But the old captain had never seen anyone foolish enough, or clever enough, to survive the wilds of Kokivorosdos Island for a little quartz.... The captain tucked the clipboard under his arm and moved to climb the gangplank. He looked around the chattering passengers. They were all either priests-in-training or contractors going for work at the mines. The captain looked over to his first mate and motioned his hand. The sailor, who looked to be a demi, saluted and climbed down towards the engine room while the Wolus stood at the edge of the ship. Reaching into his tunic the captain pulled out a brass whistle that he put to his lips. When he blew, the sharp sound rang through the air, over all present voices.

"Right, now that I have yer attentions... I'm only gunna say this once. Don't fight on me ship, don't spit or shit on me ship, and listen to my orders and I won't throw you overboard. My name's Vafri and I'm the captain of the Grani. We're riding to Kokivorosdos Isle. It'll be a twenty minute trip, but that's twenty minutes I gotta deal with ya. I don't wanna bring back any corpses so stay in the settlements within the island and I won't be. Don't let me hear ah Barghrest dregged yer arses through the woods." With that Captain Vafri stepped down and the ship's horns blew, warning nearby sailors they were setting off.

# CHAPTER FOURTEEN

## Nah Na Na Na

For the second time Pandora found himself on the deck of a boat sailing across the sea. Luckily, this time, it was only a few miles to land and he had company.

"So Rika decided not to come?" That had been Mara's question when they boarded. It seemed that they had packed up and were about to set off with Cardinal Hash, but the salamander went down the hall towards the toilet and never returned. They had to go before the boat left so had no choice but to leave without her. It left Pandora wondering if Rika had ever planned on going with them. Pandora has come to understand the woman found public spaces as difficult as he did, but unlike her he didn't lack experience in dealing with it. He had to learn to speak with the public at an early age. He was often taken into town with the monks during the afternoon prayers.

In the religion of Oikos, prayer was a regular part of life. Faithfuls would pray in the morning before going into the fields to work or heading off to begin their morning errands. They would pray again at midday when people went home to eat with their families, or spouses brought lunch to the men in the field so they could fill their bellies. When home they would pray again in order to show thanks for being able to safely return home. At last, during the evening meal, they would again pray in thanks for being able to have food on the table. In the city he barely found time to pray so since arriving it was difficult to head out into town to pray for others and help them with their blessings, but it seemed Artimmus faithfuls only prayed at night. On certain days and holidays they would hold mass which allowed the members of the faith to gather and pray together in order to strengthen the blessings. It was believed that when more faithfuls prayed they would be able to increase the power of a blessing making it more effective.

He was used to praying with others, having conversations, but he sure didn't enjoy doing it. Even so, it seemed to make others happy. It made the brothers happy as well. They were always worried about him because he was always so small and thin when compared to them. He was the first Avius they had seen on the island so it was difficult to be sure if he was healthy in his youth. Even now he wondered because Hash was quite large and even Ash, whom they were traveling with, had significant height when they stood side by side.

"Yeah...." Pandora felt a little sad. He wanted to know a bit more about Rika. She seemed to keep a lot to herself. "We'll have to try our best." Pandora was looking out towards the sea while he spoke. During his first trip he didn't get the chance to appreciate the ocean. He sulked a bit. "Maybe this time I can get some good sleep." He wanted to nap before they arrived. Mara was standing at his side, listening to his woes. The Drakus twitched the end of her tail before she looked down towards Pan's free hand. She moved to slide her hand into his, feeling quite proud of her sneaky move, but before she could complete her plot to take hold of his hand she was met with an interruption.

"Ser Pandora! Ser Mara, there you are." Ash's soft voice called out to them as he struggled to weave through the boisterous crowd. They were only five minutes at sea and people were already starting to drink. Managing to finally squeeze through it would appear the young owl Avius had three tankards in hand. "They were handing out some drinks and I got us some!" The young man seemed quite proud of himself and handed a tankard to Mara and Pan, of which they accepted. Mara sniffed at the liquid inside the mug only to sneer and turn her head away as her lips curled up in disgust. Pan chuckled, noticing Mara's reaction. She looked to have a good sense of smell, but one didn't really need one because even he could smell the metal tinge at the edge of the drink's profile and he hadn't put his nose to the cup yet.

"Where did you even get these...?" Pandora tried not to make a face at the offered drink, but he was sure it wasn't something he could stomach. He looked over to Ash. The corners of his beak pulled up as he smiled and held out the mug he clutched in his claws, out towards Pandora.

"Some of the contractors were sharing it among the training priests." The bird tilted his head, eyes pinching closed in a smile. "You see after our oaths we will not be able to drink anymore so they wanted to send us off with a memory." While Ash spoke Mara inched towards the edge of the ship and poured the drink overboard, behind the owl's back. Pandora glanced over and chuckled before turning his attention to Ash who looked over his shoulder at Mara who was clutching the now empty mug, blinking at the pair. The young owl looked back to Pandora and parted his beak. "Oh no -- I-I'm sorry are you not allowed to drink?" Pandora glanced to the side.

"I don't have any oaths against it, but I don't prefer it." he looked back into the mug where the murky liquid sat, rippling whenever he moved. "What kind of drink is this anyway? It smells -- ah, strong." That was more polite than the word he was thinking. To Pandora it was a putrid scent that made the back of his throat itch. Ash blinked his eyes and would chuckle.

"You are a strange one ser Pandora. Don't you recognize it?" Ash raised the mug, hooking his beak over the edge and taking a heavy swig. The bird made quick work of the drink. The feathers on his throat seemed to puff up as he chugged down the uncharming mixture of booze and rotten meat. It was not a drink that was commonly found on the islands. It was said that Wolus had all sorts of dishes involving meat, including drinks and bread. Of course these rumors were based on the old stories of the race's origin as predators. In the past the consumption of meat was commonplace, but as more and more of the groups began to live together most meats were limited by lack of access to open land to raise animals they hunted for before the construction of cities, villages, and towns. They say it was civilization that bred the strength of prey-type Tierans and put them in positions of power that the predatory races once had a stranglehold of.

"Meat liquor!" A masculine voice called out. From the crowd of drinking trainees and contractors stepped out a tall, demi male. He had dark skin and a long black tail hanging from his red trousers. Over his white robes he wore a red cloak with white accents. He stood on plantigrade paws covered in well-made leather sandals. The sandals were a beautiful mahogany color with silver buttons that held down the straps over his feet. His hair was a deep hazel and braided back. The end of the braid was held tied by a red, silk ribbon. The man appeared to be an otter Mustus by his webbed fingers and his rounded, webbed toes. "After our vows we won't get this chance again. And here you are wasting a perfectly curated chance. Ash here was so nice to deliver you some even if you're an Oikos wastrel." He began to laugh, the men flanking his sides adding to the mirth with their own chortles.

"Do I know you?" Pandora didn't ask for a speech or a spring of insults because he wasn't willing to ingest rotting meat. Now that he knew what it was he realized why he recognized the smell. It was something long burned into his memory. "Not that it matters. I didn't ask for the drink, but I'm not ungrateful, so here. You could drink it." He held up the mug, offering it to the Mustus. The otter demi pulled his lips back in a contentious expression. Raising his left hand, his right still clutching his mug, he would smack the drink from Pandora's hand, sending the wretched fluid splattering to the ground as the wooden tankard bounced upon hitting the deck. The cup rolled across the ground before finally meeting the edge of the floor where it tumbled down into the ocean. The otter pulled his hand back up, ready to bring his fist down at Pan, but would stop when Mara moved to stand at his side, protectively.

"My name is Nanaeh. Nanaeh Grassweaver." The otter boasted, puffing out his chest and moving to rest his hand on his hip. "I'm the heir of the Grassweaver family. Top of my class at Chrysus Cathedral." He grinned smugly. "You, you're a heretic aren't you. A Drakus." He pointed his claw tipped finger at Mara who had been idly taking in Pandora's scent. He smelled much better than those drinks and she found herself wanting to sink her fangs into his neck instead, pin him down and... "You're going to be my woman!"

# CHAPTER FIFTEEN

## Let Me Pin You Down

Mara had been lost in her thoughts. The scent of the drink not only stung her nose but it made her feel a little seasick. She had decided to lean in close to Pandora and alter her point of focus. When she caught his scent, which was leagues more pleasant than that rotten gunk, she found herself wanting to take advantage of his distraction. She noticed when he spoke the muscles along his neck stretched and flexed in a way that drew her eyes. His body was frail looking, but he had beaten her soundly in that moment. Her instincts kicked in and she would attempt to get his attention in order to show him she was available.

"You're going to be my woman!" The words almost sounded like snapping branches, the irritating voice clicking between her ear holes. She slowly turned her gaze towards the Mustus Tieran, finally realizing he was standing still there. She had seen him approach and felt intuitively irritated by them so chose to ignore them. The Drakus was more determined to pin Pandora down and let him have his way with her. "Move out the way!" Nanaeh motioned his hand dismissively at the raven Avius. Pandora moved to point to himself before he looked between Mara and Ash. Ash raised his claw, waving as if to brush the eyes off him. "All of you! I'm taking that woman for myself." He stared at

Pandora who stayed standing there. Ash had already retreated and tucked away into the growing crowd. "Are you listening? Move!" He moved to shove Pandora.

Pandora did not feel he was someone who was easily bothered by a situation. But he really didn't like violence and so when he was attacked he reacted accordingly. When Nanaeh's hand came swinging down he would throw his hand up to intercept it, he caught the man's fist in his open palm before closing his hand over it. He stomped his foot down on Nanaeh's sandal as he raised his other hand to slam his palm flat against his chest before shoving the man back.

"Hey!" The Rodrus demi standing beside Nanaeh jumped forward in order to lunge at Pandora, but Mara moved to shoulder check the man. When he threw himself at the raven Avius she lowered herself to a slight crouch so she had her shoulder leveled with his chest. She charged at the demi with all her strength and slammed herself into his chest with enough force that he was thrown back and sent flying to the ground. "Augh!" The rat Rodrus hit the ground and slid across the deck and into the guardrails.

"You lizard!" The other demi on Nanaeh's side would shout out and go to grab Pandora by the collar of his tunic, lifting him off the ground. This demi appeared to be a Rodrus as well, but much larger in build than the other demi, who had black hair, than this one who had white. He was not muscular, but his strength stood out seeing as he was able to lift another man off the ground. He pulled back his fist, but before he was able to, Pan had raised his talons and slammed it against his chest, gripping down in a grabbing motion to pinch and pull his cloth and skin beneath. "Aah!" When he shouted out in pain Mara would step forward and push her right palm into her left fist before jamming her left elbow in his side. The white-haired demi crumpled to the floor. Pan landed on the ground and would tumble back, but Mara stood behind him to catch him against her chest.

"What are you doing?!" Nanaeh shouted and pushed to his feet, his body a little heavy from his previous drinking. Speaking of, it seems when he was thrown back his mug was sent flying across the ship. "Why are you fighting for this weakling? Let him fight for himself!" Pandora looked at his hands and wondered just how strong he really was. The Mustus was right. He had been unable to stand up against the Rodrus a few days ago and worried he could make a blunder like that again.

"Cowards!" Mara called out as the rest of the passengers watched with interest. They called out as the fight proceeded and watched as things wound up between the men of the cloth. "Even if I were interested, there's no way I'd conceded my attention to some cowards who can't fight without ganging up on one person!"

"What?!" Nanaeh spat at. "This is my romp! I have every right to ask for their help!" He leaned forward and brushed his hands down his robe before shaking his head. "And what do you mean? How are you not interested in me?!" At his question the crowd began to laugh. It seems only Nanaeh was unaware as to just what it was that made him unattractive. Mara would snub her nose and take Pandora by the hand before she turned to walk away, tugging the monk with her. Pan looked back at the otter Mustus as he followed the Drakus. Soon they were out of sight. "Tsk....what was that?!" Nanaeh turned his head to the group of passengers that was now dispersing with the conflict settled.

"It was strange." The owl Avius stepped out from the thinning collective. Ash pressed his fingers to his feathered chin in thought. This was the first time he has heard of a Drakus turning down a suitor, let alone jumping in to defend someone else.

"You said that girl was a heretic, that she had no scruples!" Nanaeh stamped his foot down as he complained, now just among Ash and his entourage of goons. Ash motioned his clawed hands in an attempt to soothe the irritated Mustus.

"Now, now. She is. But I am as surprised as you that she stepped in. It is probably best if you try and talk to the female alone and get her to agree that way. She might view him affectionately because he is so small." Ash has noticed that Pandora knew nothing about this trip or else he wouldn't have agreed to his uncle's preening about the self-satisfying pride of succeeding at the Ranch's tests.

In reality that place was a hellish zone of despair and Ash would do everything it took to get rid of those who were going to get in his way. If this kept Nanaeh busy with Pan he didn't have too much to worry about as Nanaeh was the second most influential one at the Ranch, second only to him. The owl Avius appeared to be thinking. Ash would look over to Nanaeh once he settled on an idea.

"Drakus female are bound by their sense of strength, just show her yours." But it seemed she also favored the monk and he wanted to find out why. If he could get this idiot to push the envelope and get him and the monk kicked off the island he could handle two of his problems in one step.

"That won't be a problem." Nanaeh assured Ash. "You just keep letting me know what they're up to and I'll take that heretic girl and teach her to be a good little follower!" Below deck Mara had found the sleeping quarters and would secure a room for Pan and herself. Pandora stepped into the room and looked back as Mara closed the door. He smirked, feeling his exhaustion catching up with him.

"You didn't have to do that, Mara." Pandora moved to sit on the edge of the cot after he set aside his knapsack. He sighed. "I was about to leave the conflict anyway." Mara walked over to the cot and shoved Pandora onto the bedding. He didn't resist her action so laid himself down. Mara climbed over his body before laying herself down at his side. She didn't answer him. He looked over to the woman who had already closed her eyes and settled her head on his shoulder and scooched closer against him. Seeing he was too tired to fight it Pandora would also drift off to sleep.

It seemed to happen all over again for Pandora. As Mara roused from her slumber she would stretch out her body in a way that imposed on his smaller form. He was just glad Mara was about his size and he could easily wrap his arms around her waist were he to need to. In fact he would do just that. Resting his hands on her hips he would try and hold her away from his body so she wasn't rubbing all over him. Even he noticed that whenever she did this he caught traces of her scent all over his body and while at the Ranch he would rather not be accused of having inappropriate relations with Mara when they did nothing more than rest together.

The boat arrived at Kokivorosdos Island with no further incidents from the passengers. The priests and contractors disembarked upon arrival. The would-be miners had a wagon waiting for them on the docks. They would board the back of the carriage and were soon carried away down the dirt road. The training priests walked down a dirt path from the dock. They would travel along for ten minutes before arriving at the front gates of the ranch where a tall, demi Wolus stood with their hand resting atop their rancher's cap. They appeared to be wearing a brown tunic that was tucked into their trousers. White swathing cloth were wrapped tightly around their ankles and a pair of leather foot coverings.

"Weeeelcome to Red Geode Ranch!" A loud, cheerful voice would greet the training priests. "My name's Frei Forestwalker. My family's run operations on this island for over five generations! I'll be walking with you through your duties and expectations so I wanna make sure you listen to our helpers and we'll have a great time!" Frei stepped aside and held out their hand towards the ranch. There near the entrance were the helpers they mentioned. "These fellas will be taking you to your cabins. They'll be where you'll be staying for the month with your fellow ardents. In an hour we'll be having orientation so take your time to settle and have a look around. Just make sure not to leave the Ranch's property. It ain't safe beyond the gates, what with the wild animals!" With that Frei would depart, leaving the helpers to take the designated groups to their cabins.

# CHAPTER SIXTEEN

## Trials Of The Ranch

The men and women were kept in separate cabins. The ranch was separated into a few different areas. First were the stalls, barn, and arena where they trained and kept a number of the domesticated animals used in pulling carts or supplying milk to the facility. All the animals were trained to climb up and down the mountain paths with their cargo to deliver mining equipment to the camps that dotted the mountain. The most valuable animal in the stalls were ever intrepid Coursers. These six legged ungulates had short, grabbing noses and forward facing eyes. They were at home in the mountains and could carry over half of their body weight which accounted for a weighed down cart full of equipment. The other animals that could be found in the barns were Capers, horned mountain-borne mammals prized for their milk, as well as the versatile Pullets which were domesticated fowl that laid large eggs and were sometimes slaughtered for their meat. Along with other common barnyard animals raised for slaughter these were the few large ones found, as it was difficult to raise grazing animals on an island. Beyond the animal pens were the cabins, rancher's homestead, and a fishing pond filled with water fowl and Rana, croaking frog-like creatures. Beyond that was a great lodge where the miners met in the evening for dinner and rest, but it was beyond a fence and out of bounds for the training priests, or so the helpers had told them.

The helpers all appeared to be Rodrus that were garbed in the Ranch's signature uniform which consisted of a set of a brown tunic and grey trousers with a jacket overtop that kept the ranchers protected against the animals and environment they dealt with daily. They had the same wide brim hats that kept them warm and dry during the overcast or rainy days. These were the individuals the priests would be looking to for their daily tasks and the rules. They have helped at the ranch since they were young and Frei's family have taken care of the island for generations. In cabin one, Pandora would be settled with Ash, Nanaeh, his goons and a few other priests. This year was a particularly small party. Pandora looked over to the helper who was explaining things.

"Yeah there were at least three cabins full of training priests." The helper explained. "The year before that we actually ran out of room and had to drag in extra cots!" He laughed and pointed out the important features of the room. "There's a shower in the back of the cabin. Each of your beds has a lockbox for your private items and for meals we'll be meeting at the homestead's main house for breakfast and dinner. For lunch the women of the house bring the meals to everyone while they're out in the fields. Make sure you guys sleep well since you'll have early mornings and late nights." He tapped his chin trying to remember if there was anything else. "Ah, be sure to meet at the barn in an hour. Can't miss it. It's the big red building that smells like animals." He laughed and would leave them to settle in.

"Well, I'm not staying." Nanaeh dropped his knapsack onto his bed and removed his outer robes, leaving him in his tunic and trousers. "You guys can roam around, but I'm going to familiarize myself with our companions." He would say while running his hands back through his hair, his round ears bouncing back up after he let go. Nanaeh turned to leave. His two goons looked back at the other priests and would wave, chuckling to themselves as they followed the Mustus out. The other priests talked among each other, feeling they should follow in the man's footsteps because it would be just a short few weeks before they were priests and locked away from all the major pleasures of the world. Feeling Nanaeh was in the right, the other priests would get up and go follow the man's example. Pandora was in his own thoughts and worked on locking up his knapsack in the footlocker before turning to face the door as the priests poured out of the cabin. Ash and another priest looked to have stayed behind to finish unpacking.

"Don't mind him..." Ash turned to face Pandora. Ash had dressed down into a simple pair of robes and his trousers. "We're all a little sad about leaving behind our lives for this new one. But think of all the people we'll be helping? I'm going to go look at the animals." He raised his hand and turned to leave. The other priest didn't say anything and also left. Pandora sighed. Of course he was the last one out, but that was okay. Pandora would put on a red, long sleeved tunic. His pants were their usual black short tights. It was easy for him to move around in and since he was on an island full of nothing but priests there really was no need to advertise he was a monk. Shifting his weight he would stretch and make his way outside.

Nanaeh had already made his way to cabin four, where the women were staying. The women settled in quite quickly. They seemed to be in good spirits about the pilgrimage.

"I didn't know that..." Mara would say as she stepped out of the cabin. She changed into a more familiar dress that was a pale red with white accents. One of the women loaned it to her after the Drakus spoke of her preference. She preferred wearing a dress over the skirts that they seemed to have a lot of at Silver Church. "So even a heretic like me....?"

"Of course!" The woman giggled. "This would be considered one of your ten rites that you're expected to do before being allowed to return to the religion." She looked to be a young ferret Mustus kin with black paws, a black mask and almost white, creme colored coat of fur. "All heretics have to meet the ten rites to return to a religion after being labeled a heretic. But it's easier for you. You didn't break any laws right? You were just born in the Deadlands! It's way easier for them to return! I'm sure your boyfriend would be so proud!"

"Oh, n-no--" Mara felt on edge when people assumed Pandora was her boyfriend. He wasn't even her type! "He's not my boyfriend." Some of the girls let out sad sounding coos.

"It's okay honey! He'll come around!" One woman praised.

"Oh yes," Another agreed. "He's a Oikos Monk, isn't he? So lucky." As those of Oikos were allowed to be bonded together and participate in handfasting ceremonies.

"You just need a little push!" Another woman cheered. While the women seemed to endear themselves to Mara's saga, Nanaeh watched. Hearing such things displeased him. There was no way that she was going to attach herself to that monk, not while he was here and he'd make sure of it. Clearing his throat Nanaeh stepped out into the open. He put his hand on his chest and strode out of his cover with his head held high.

"If it isn't the lovely Mara!" Mara turned to the sound of Nanaeh's voice. It was like the buzzing of a bug wrestling in tall grass. The woman turned her head from the man and scoffed. "Now, don't turn away from me yet. I've already decided I'm going to prove to you that I am strong and capable enough to be your partner. In fact... I am going to get top of class during these lessons." Those like Nanaeh were not just bark with no bite though. His kind were extremely strong and their sharp claws were said to be able to cut through wood with ease. Otter Mustus were known to have dexterous paws that could rival even an Ursus' nimble digits when it came to the arts.

"Leave Mara alone Nanaeh!" A woman called.

"Aren't you a Grassweaver!? Why are you even a priest?!" Another looked to call him out on his family name. The Grassweaver family was a well known family on the northern coasts along the mainland. They were a competent family of artisans who had always bred great figures that contributed to the crafting arts. In fact Nanaeh's father was known for the construction of the very cranes they used in Mene and had restructured the entire shipping industry in the matter of a day!

"Don't bring my family into this!" Nanaeh threw out his hand. "This is my decision!" He stamped his sandal covered foot on the ground. "You girls giggle all you want! I'll show you the strength of a Grassweaver!" Frustrated Nanaeh would turn on his heel and stomp away. His two Rodrus companions snapped their heads up when Nanaeh stormed off and scampered after him.

"Don't worry too much about him... though." One of the women sighed. "They say it happens a lot here. Honestly that's how my mom had me! She came to the Ranch to finish her studies but left pregnant with me~!"

"Oh come off it." Another woman dismissed the tall tale. "Pregnancy doesn't happen that fast. Don't exaggerate." They would laugh.

# CHAPTER SEVENTEEN

## Insert Foot

It wasn't difficult to see that Mara was a fine specimen of her species. Drakus were not common outside of the Deadlands and were all but unheard of in the Northern coasts. She had wide thighs and a thick tail that were good for swimming, but it was her cerulean scales that stood out and contrasted against her delicately peach-colored skin. Her dual-toned hair stood out as well. Though blue tones of hair were quite common among water Drakus, having a second hair color among the tendrils was a unique touch hard to ignore. She wasn't as tall as other Drakus either which made her immediately more approachable than those of her kind. All Drakus were born within the Deadlands because of their preference of living on and near coastal cliffs. It was an ancient territory for them, but unlike other groups who had left their territories for the greater expanses of fertile land and civilization those that chose to remain in the Deadlands were considered to have abandoned society as a whole.

The simple fact was that all the lands in the Deadlands were considered the territory of the old king who shunned the goddesses and society's change from the Old Ways. The land is said to be cursed, infertile and a ripe breeding ground for monsters.

Some of the other male priests arrived at cabin four, looking to see if they could take their chance to flirt with the women. While the men chatted with the women of the priesthood, Nanaeh could only watch from a distance as he had already made his tactical retreat. He stood with his arms crossed over his chest, brows furrowed as he stared at Mara who seemed subdued when socializing with the group, yet she was adored by the women and fawned over. The male priests thought it better to avoid a dangerous situation. They had been in the crowd and witnessed how easily Pandora and Mara had taken Nanaeh down. As for the collective there was not much variation in their races. The majority of those present appeared to be Mustus or Rodrus, which were the most common family branches in the region due to their large family units. In fact two of the women were cousins and one of the men was a distant nephew to Nanaeh himself, but the man seemed more mild-mannered in his nature.

"How are ya gunna get close to her now...?" Nanaeh's black-haired Rodrus lackey questioned, his round ears drooping at the expression the otter demi was making. He seemed frustrated and out of ideas on how to approach the Drakus. The white-haired Rodrus demi seemed to be watching the crowd, peering around the tree in the direction of the cabin. Nanaeh had his back pushed up against another tree with his black haired companion sitting on the ground watching him.

"Oy, she's leavin'!" The white-haired goon barked as his fleshy tail seemed to stand up on end at the surprise. By the looks of it Mara had bid the other women farewell and she would step down from the deck of the cabin. Her soft pads silently touched against the grass, her tail still dragging behind her along the steps. She tilted her head at the feeling beneath her toes. Grass. Grass seemed to be a common ground covering in the camp but it still gave her a strange feeling she couldn't quite accept. She grew up on the tall, sandy shoals of the coastal cliffs in the southern edges of the mainland's islands. Her family spent most of their time migrating along the coast, mostly in water. It was why, despite the rough terrain of her environment, she never grew hard pads. Even when they did have to travel on land she would always ride on her father's shoulders. Even the soil was soft to the touch.

Mara separated from the group and made her way down the dirt path that led through the cabins, towards the port they had arrived at. She would recall there were some other buildings down that way. The scent of animals was clear to her nose. As she made her way down the path she would notice some of the helpers working. One was walking a group of waterfowl from the pond towards some open grassfields. Others were doing repairs to the various buildings and some weeding along the paths, collecting the plucked plants to be used later to feed the herbivorous livestock. All the while Nanaeh would follow Mara from a distance. He had sent his lackeys off to distract the little monk. It was only a few moments after Mara left the cabin to look around that Ash had approached Nanaeh's group. He said Pandora was only just leaving the cabin and they had a chance. This left Ash with his chance.... While Nanaeh stalked Mara he moved to approach cabin four.

"Ah, h-hey, have any of you seen Pandora?" The owl Avius looked around and blinked his large eyes, pushing up his claws to adjust his glasses. The others looked over to the worried looking owl who had his free claw come to rest against his chest. "Ah... well he didn't look too well and when everyone said they were coming here -- I'm sorry I just thought...?" The people looked between each other to talk before turning their attention to Ash. "I just thought he would come with me to see the critters." The man moved to take a step back and clasp his hands together. "Wait, where's Nanaeh--?"

"Well, he left when Mara rejected him again." One of the women announced.

"You don't think he went to harass the little guy again?" A stouter male seemed concerned, but there really wasn't much they could do. There was a distinct hierarchy. A few of the training priests were from poor districts and couldn't really afford to get on the bad side of someone with Grassweaver as a name. "What about you? You're a Silverchanger, aren't you Ash?" He would ask. Ash would sputter.

"I-I am but my family aren't brutes or anything. You guys think I can stand up to someone like Nanaeh that has muscles coming out of his tail?" He seemed to wheeze a bit. "Besides, he's a Grassweaver. If he wanted he could just make any of us disappear." The owl insisted. "I heard his father helped get him into the priesthood in the first place." For people like them it seemed like too much. They spent their lives studying and they had entire generations who wore the cloth as a sign of humility, yet people like Nanaeh made a joke of their hard work.

"It isn't right..." Another man spoke. "You shouldn't just use your name to push others around...."

"What about you Ash?" One of the men asked. "Doesn't it bother you? It wasn't until they made that law that they let people from Artisan houses join the clergy." It was an insult to them that the rich could just buy their way into things.

"I know you're upset..." Ash tried to calm their nerves. "I am too... but maybe we can show him how hard it is being a priest so he understands. My uncle said it's our job to test our fellows to ensure they are strong enough for what the evils of the world would throw at them." The others listened to Ash with intense interest. Meanwhile the Ranch went along as usual. Frei was in the barn, sweeping up with some of their helpers. A shadow crept up at the edge of the entrance that caused their head to snap up.

"Who's there?!" Frei had to be careful because even domesticated animals could sometimes be ornery and get someone hurt.

Pandora peeked into the barn, looking around. He recalled Ash saying he was going to look at the animals, but he saw neither hide nor feather of the owl. "Oh! Well if'n isn't the little bird. You're early, lad. Well don't stand there! Come on in and pick up a broom!" Pandora would nod his head and look around. One of the helpers would hand him a broom and he would get to helping sweep up the hay. "So what brings a stray over to the barn so early? Don't get along with yer fellows?!"

"Oh, something like that." Pandora grunted. "I'm an ardent of Oikos, so I've already done my rites. I'm just accompanying the church's nephew as part of my pilgrimage." The helpers paused in their chores and looked over to Pandora. Frei reached up to adjust their hat, a little surprised by the response.

"Really, really?" Frei laughed. "Well go figure. That's such a nice thing to do! What a good boy!" Frei walked over and moved to ruffle Pandora's hair. "Well I know! Why don't you help me hang the banner to welcome the others! This is like a mini pilgrimage for these kids. I'm here to make it pretty difficult for them so they don't turn out to be lil shits. How about you be my little helper bird?"

"Sounds a little strange." Pandora would admit. The way the Wolus spoke was a bit strange. It wasn't an accent he was used to hearing them speak in. Usually Wolus were more eloquent with their words and enunciated well. "I don't mind, but why do you give them a hard time? Aren't they here to learn?" Pandora had many thoughts concerning the various practices the church had, and just as few answers.

"Well it's simple." Frei had no problem confessing their role in everything. "You Oikos lot, you work a lot with the common folk, right? Pray out there." Frei motioned their hand only for Pandora to nod in confirmation. "You gotta hunt your own food, grow your own vegetables, right?" Again Pandora would nod. "These kids spent most of their lives studying in cushy academies. Schools provided the food, the clothing, even all the basics like laundry and cleaning are done by slaves. This is where reality gives them a swift kick in the pants. The government decided on this program three decades ago after a priest was charged with murder."

"What?" Pandora stared at Frei. "What happened?" It wasn't something Pan was expecting to hear. Misguided advice, poorly memorized hymns was the reach of the monk's assumptions. But murder...?

"Oh ya, ya." Frei nodded. "Mistook a fear-stricken parishioner with a cut purse. Feeling priests had no worldly experience, they're brought 'em to my family's Ranch." Though it made sense that a monk or even priest should have knowledge of the world they were trying to protect, Pan had a sinking feeling there was much more to the story than what Frei had told him.

# CHAPTER EIGHTEEN

## Pecking Order

It was time for the orientation. The male and female priests gathered together at the barn. Pandora was already there so he was settled among the stools that had been put out specifically for the gathering. The attendants were surprised by not only the spaciousness in the barn, but its cleanliness. Pandora and the workers had done a good job making sure everything was prepared. One by one all of the training priests would enter the space and find a seat they could comfortably settle at. Mara stepped in among the women. She had arrived earlier but had stopped to look around the utilities, including what looked to be the stalls they kept the Coursers in. She was quickly able to spot Pan among the crowd and moved to seat herself beside him. The action made some of the women giggle encouragingly as they too found places to settle comfortably among the men. Frei would step up onto a raised stage which was set up just for the orientation.

"Howdy! Like I said before when you were disembarking, my name's Frei and I'll be the one givin' you yer tasks for the next foreseeable month! We'll be doing work at the Ranch and up at the mines. While you'll be free to wander during free hours, under no circumstance are you to leave the Ranch. Make sure you're always within eyesight of me or the helpers. You're gunna learn the hard way life don't always go the way ya want." The orientation continued in this manner. The training priests were told they would need to depend on their wit, problem-solve and manage their own laundry, meals, and chores. The most helpers would be aiding them with would be the animals and heavy equipment to make sure they didn't break bones or the machines. While Frei spoke, Mara turned her attention to Pandora as she sat beside him. The raven Avius sat leaned back with his leg pulled up over his knee. He turned his gaze over to the Drakus and arched his brow. She opened her mouth to say something, but Frei's voice interrupted her attempt. "Alright! We're gunna assign yer groups and we're gunna be off to the stalls. We're gunna have you lot saddle your very own Coursers!"

Frei led the group of priests out of the barn and along the path towards the stalls. Mara moved to keep up with Pan. She reached out her hand towards his swaying arm, but Nanaeh stepped in her path and held out his paw, offering her stable footing on the rough walkway. Mara snubbed her nose and moved to walk to the front of the pack, Pandora watching her pass by. He looked back towards where Nanaeh stood with his hands on his hips, glaring in the Avius' direction. Pandora hadn't noticed Mara reaching for him because Ash had taken his attention.

"I'm sorry you missed me." The owl Avius apologized. "I thought you would have liked the Coursers and went to find you, but it seems you had come to find me." He chuckled. "By the way, Nanaeh hasn't bothered you again, has he?" Pandora tilted his head. After the otter Mustus left the cabin he didn't see him anywhere, but he also wasn't looking for him.

"It's alright. I'm not really interested in him." Pandora's words caused Ash to cock his head slightly in confusion. "Well --" Pandora laughed softly, the talking crowd around him a comfort because they weren't looking to him for prayer or working miracles. They were just other folk of the cloth having a day out.

"We're here to work and Nanaeh seems to be looking to foster a different kind of relationship." Though he was sure it would fail because Mara was a stubborn kind of person who seemed to carry a predilection for people who were independent and could handle their own responsibilities. "What about you? I've seen you trying to avoid him once or twice." Even during the conflict on the boat Ash vanished like a ghost among the crowd. Pan didn't hold it against him because he would have done the same had he a choice.

"Well..." Ash rubbed the back of his neck, ruffling his feathers. "I didn't plan on doing anything. Nanaeh's behavior seems to have flustered the rest of the clergy here. They are intent on ..." He glanced over. Nanaeh had moved to the side of the group with his two goons, the three talking and watching Mara. Pan followed his gaze, but thought nothing of it for now. "I don't want to get involved, but it seems the others feel Nanaeh should be taught a lesson. I'm worried they'll go too far." Pandora turned his attention to Ash. What did he mean? "Well I'm sure my uncle warned you. When you come to the Ranch it's to teach yourself humility as a priest. Nanaeh is very proud because he comes from the Grassweaver family. They are a powerful family of Artisans who basically paid his way into the seminary academy."

"Alright, eyes front!" Frei called for everyone's attention. "This is a Courser." They would grip the reins that were attached to the beast's bridle and pull them out of the stall. It was a large animal that had two front legs and four back legs, six altogether. Most Courser were a solid color, but this one appeared to be piebald in color with black on its hind quarters and much of his head and neck area a silver-grey. It had a short, flexible nose that allowed it to grab the branches of low to the ground shrubs in order to strip them of their vegetation. Atop their heads were long, triangular ears that moved around with caution as the warbling crowd gasped in awe at the beast. It wasn't an animal typically seen in cities as the choice beasts of burden were large, domesticated cattle called Bos. "Now the important thing is that these here

Courser smell fear. If you so much as flinch they'll be sure to spit you between the eyes and bite ya. So, anyone want to handle it first?" They held out the leather strap.

"You know..." Pandora stared ahead at the beast before taking a step forward, away from Ash. "As long as no one's hurt, I think it's okay to argue a little." They always argued about things at the monastery. Whether it was about how to use the donations or who got to sleep on the bed closest to the window during the summer. Those arguments led to them airing out ideas they wouldn't have previously considered. In the end they would come to an agreement and all would be well because everyone had been able to get their feelings across and feel heard. "I'll try." Pandora would be the first to approach Frei, who handed him off the reins. Nanaeh stepped up behind Ash to speak, but the owl held up his claws before clasping his hands in front of his chest and sighing.

"*Don't worry.*" Ash whispered. "*It seems the monk doesn't know his place. After the first task he'll be knocked down a few pegs. I'll give that to you as an opportunity.*" He glanced over to Mara. "*She doesn't seem to have a close relationship with him yet.*" Nanaeh seemed pleased by this news.

"Alright!" Frei nodded, pleased. "So each of you'll be pairing up and saddling up a Courser then we're gunna walk them out to the arena to walk 'em around. Let's go!" Frei clapped their hands and would let the helpers come around to keep an eye on things. "Remember, don't hesitate!" But there was a lot of trouble with these young training priests who had spent their lives in the dormitories. They had never handled animals, let alone see ones this big up close! "Don't back up! Show 'im who's boss!" The helpers assisted the priests in handling the animals.

Some of the young trainees were still working on pairing up. While Pandora acted as an example for the others, Nanaeh moved in to get close and grabbed Mara by her arm, gripping down firmly. At first she had thought it was Pandora, but quickly realized he had gone to the front already. When she looked to her side it was Nanaeh. She clenched her right hand into a fist.

"Don't try it, or else I'll really show you why I have these." He snapped his fangs at her. Though small they were the teeth of a predator and he moved to pull her to his side forcibly. "Listen, you're gunna let me show you right. How about we ride the Courser together and you can hold onto my waist." He curled his hand in a way that his claws dug against her scales, but it didn't have the impression he hoped because her scales were a lot coarser than he had thought they would be. "Why are your scales so hard? Haven't been in the water lately? See I'm a swimmer so you can always have fun with me in the water. These muscles aren't just for fighting you see... come on. It's easier if you just give in to my charms." Mara moved to pull her arm from his grip but he reached up behind her and pulled back her hair, forcing her to step back and line up with the rest of the group. "Heretics should behave. You don't want to get the little monk kicked off the island, do you?" Mara had pulled her claws back, ready to rip the otter's face off, but when he mentioned Pandora she would remember. She was only here because of him and if she did something that put him on the spot he wouldn't be able to finish his pilgrimage or even stay at the church because the cardinal was holding this event over him in such a manner. "Haa, good girl." Nanaeh breathed an internal sigh of relief. He was glad Ash told him about the accommodations Pandora was being given or he wouldn't have anything to hold over the Drakus as collateral. He saw her reeling back her arm too! Yikes! He didn't need his precious face scarred up before he made it big!

# CHAPTER NINETEEN

## I'm In Charge

After a bit of trouble, and only one biting incident, they were finally able to get the Coursers into the arena. Pandora was already mounted on the stallion and looked around the paired group to realize he was the only one without a partner, but that was because Frei capitalized on his competence. Pandora was quite familiar with animals. Stray animals in the village were quite common and seeing beasts of burden pulling carts where he had been either requested to hold them for the merchant or pray for them so they would get over an injury or illness was a fundamental part of his work as a monk. To say his experience with animals was advanced was a bit overboard, but he was confident that if he was bitten he could get aid so the idea never bothered him. Because of this natural confidence animals usually felt comfortable around Pandora. He had a calm air about him that quickly put at ease most people's nerves.

Pandora noticed Mara was in the crowd and they looked to be getting along well enough. The Drakus was looking off to the side and seemed to be keeping her distance. It seemed quite a change from before where she was actively engaging with the women. When he moved to turn the Courser it stopped. Frei had grabbed its bridle.

"Where ya goin' birdie? Come on." They called. "Need ya ta show this mess over here how to sit on the saddle." The rancher tugged at the bridle and led Pandora's Courser towards some other priests who were starting to stress out the helpers who were attempting to help them into the saddles. While Pandora helped play the role of exemplary student Mara was questioned by the women. Nanaeh stood with his chest out.

"Of course she recognizes my skill." Nanaeh would profess as he confidently held his Courser close by the bridle as he stood with Mara close to his side, his free arm around her shoulders. "We're both swimmers. It's only natural that we gravitate towards one another. Right Mara?" Mara kept her head turned away and grunted. Some of the others around them looked a little annoyed, others concerned.

"Mara doesn't look like she's having fun, Nanaeh..." The male who spoke up was Nanaeh's second nephew, once removed. "Maybe you should stop bother--" Nanaeh stamped his foot on the ground, silencing the youth.

"Who asked you Shale?!" Nanaeh barked and moved to step towards the smaller otter. Shale was a kin and had a deep black coat, similar to Nanaeh's color. Shale clasped his paws together and lowered his head. "You're not even a Grassweaver!" Shale would sputter. It wasn't as if he could help having his mother's name. Because most Mustus were unique in their behaviors and didn't share cultures among their kind, like Wolus and Ursus did, a ferret Mustus could run their clan completely different from an otter Mustus. As for Nanaeh and Shale's clans, their family was named after the strongest member in the house. Shale was unable to get the Grassweaver name because his mother, who was a Reedwhistler, showed their dominance over the household with her influence and strength.

"I-it's..." Shale pressed his paw pads together, tears growing at the edge of their eyes. "You're bullying her." He sniffled, moving his paw to his face. Some of the women had endeared themselves to Shale as he was a polite fellow that tried to discuss situations. His family had been studying as priests for a generation. In fact Shale and Nanaeh's aunt was a Cleric, one of the few in the world.

"I'm in charge here Shale!" Nanaeh snarled, behaving so sharply that his Courser reacted negatively and moved to rear up, but Nanaeh held him roughly, spooking them a bit. "You're a spineless little pup!" Finally Nanaeh's Courser couldn't take it.

"Hey, hey!" One of the helpers called at the commotion. They hurried over, and turned their attention to Nanaeh's steed. The Courser panicked and reared up. They pushed forward, pressing through the crowd. The priests shouted and hurried back, but poor Shale was shell shocked and before he could move the Courser lunged at him. The small otter was kicked and sent to the ground. Shouts of panic called Frei's attention.

"Stay here Pandora!" Frei tugged their hat down and hurried towards the trouble. The rancher rushed towards the mayhem. The helpers quickly got a handle on the Courser before it could do any real damage. The male and female priests scurried back out of the way of the kicking beast, Shale on the ground attempting to guard his tender places. The panicked shouts rang in his ears, pain burning in his side. "Move, move!" Frei let out a sharp whistle and barked out a deep call that dispersed the crowd, giving the beast some space. Finally it would calm and Frei moved to help Shale to his paws. Shale was shaken up. His robes were ruffled and his fur standing on end. "You!" He called out to a helper. "Take him to the homestead and have mom check him!" Acting quickly the chosen helped moved to pull Shale's arm over his shoulder and he walked the limping otter towards the homestead. "What happened here?!" The Wolus puffed out their chest and moved to step in front of the crowd who cowered under the predator's gaze.

"I-It was me..." Ash stepped forward, to the surprise of the others. They knew Nanaeh caused it. "I'm sorry -- I got startled, lost my grip." Frei growled at the owl.

"You'll be cleaning out the Caper's sty! You'll be lucky if that kid comes out with just a scare!" They wouldn't be sure what kind of injuries Shale would have until he was checked over. Frei cocked their head and turned back to continue lessons with the others, leaving the owl to his cowardice.

"Ash... why?" One of the female priests called out. Ash smiled weakly as Nanaeh stood tall, smiling at the backup. The rowdy Mustus reached out to grab Mara and moved to tug her out of the group.

"Come with me." He leaned close to Mara and growled. "Or else I'll tell them about Pandora." Mara glanced over to Nanaeh, questioning him. First he had said he would cause trouble for her to get Pan in trouble, but now he was asserting he had some sort of information on Pan. "Oh, don't you know? He's only here to babysit Ash. If the others find out he's not even here to work they'll get angry. We're here to work to complete our rites. It's super important for priests. A monk like Pandora here is just a joke..." Mara got angry at his words. She pulled her fist back, but before she was able to act the Rodrus lackey grabbed her forearm and Nanaeh took his chance to punch her in the stomach, the one place where she didn't have hard scales guarding her skin.

At the homestead the mother Forestwalker tended to Shale's injuries. She was a gentle, older woman. She looked to be a demi with soft, tan fur and white paws. She had the boy hold an ice pack to his forehead for a while in order to numb the spot so she could stitch the open wound over his brow. She had already rubbed antiseptic over his bruises and checked his body for broken bones. In order to check him the mother Forestwalker had him remove his robes, leaving him in his underwear. It was embarrassing and made Shale feel terribly shameful. A priest was not supposed to expose their fur and skin to others in order to maintain their humility. Shale was in tears.

"Oh don't cry sweetheart. These injuries ain't so bad." Ma Nal would hush the young otter. "Coulda been worse." But no matter what Nal said, Shale felt this was a tiresome situation. Nanaeh was like this since they were pups. He was brash, selfish, and often pushed Shale around when no one was looking. He got him hurt, in trouble, and once he was put into confinement in his home because Nanaeh had broken an important gravestone in the family shrine and blamed it on Shale. "You should stand up for yourself dear. After all there's nothing wrong with being a priest that's able to speak up for himself, right?"

"What do you mean?" Shale flinched as Ma Nal finished stitching up the wound. She brushed a cloth with antiseptic on it over the wound and smiled warmly at the young man.

"Well I mean you sat here and took my needle. I say you are plenty tough. You just gotta remember people are like needles. They can poke and prod, but they're small and bend easily under tough skin. So you don't let them get to you." Shale looked up into her gold eyes. "Oh my pups always got into arguments and ended up in this condition. You know Frei's older brother works in the mines. It took a big fight to get them to get along." Shale nodded. He clenched his paws together. He just needed to stand up to Nanaeh.

# CHAPTER TWENTY

## Enough Is Enough

The sudden strike to Mara's stomach had caught her off-guard. She felt as if her breath was stolen from her lungs as a gagging sensation caught in her throat as she struggled to cough. The edges of her eyes filled with tears as they watered from the unprovoked attack. Who the hell did this piece of shit think he was?!

Mara jerked her arm free from the Rodrus by pulling the limb close to the side of her body. Before the rat was able to react Mara raised her hand up towards her chin, while she kept her arm locked tightly to the side of her body. In a snap she whipped down her arm like a hammer and knocked the Rodrus right in his groin. White sparks lit up his field of vision as his hands instinctively came down to guard his loins. His legs crossed together so frantically that the man lost balance and crumpled to the floor as every nerve ending in his body screamed for release from the firestorm that turned his body to ice.

"What--?" Nanaeh looked over to his comrade as he collapsed only for Mara to drive her right elbow into his stomach. He felt the same breathless wheeze rattle through his lungs before a flurry of blue blurred in his vision. Mara had spun around on her heel and threw a vengeance fueled punch into Mustus' face using her left fist. Her knuckles crunched into the delicate cartilage of his nose and would have broken through to his bone had the otter stayed still, seeing Mara's fist speeding his way he had attempted to move back, only managing to avoid shattering his septum. The force was enough to drive blood from Nanaeh's nose, the ribbon of crimson fluttering in the air as he staggered back and onto his butt. He snapped his hands over his mouth and nose as the mix of mucus and blood rushed from his snout. The Drakus raised her foot and slammed it right into his face, sending him reeling back.

The crowd shouted with surprise. Pandora was finally able to ride the Courser from the other group of working priests who barely managed to get their saddles onto their beast. Pandora looked down into the crowd and would realize that Nanaeh was on the ground. The white-haired goon would jump at Mara only to be punched in the mouth and sent straight to the ground. The black-haired man was still down on the ground clutching his jewels.

"Mara? What happened?" Pandora climbed off the Courser and it would turn to the side and start grazing. Marra grinned down at the crippled trio and rushed over to Pandora, pushing into his arms. He held out his arms but moved to rest his hands on her shoulders when she wrapped her arms around his waist. He looked around. Some of the women giggled while the men watched the three writhe on the ground and felt the woman had gone too far in her reactions. One should never strike so low even if the man was a hated enemy! But they were not confident in understanding if being kicked between the legs was ever a worthwhile punishment.

"They attacked me, Pan!" She nuzzled her head against his and gripped his hips tight. Pandora looked over to the fallen priests before he would move to step forward. He feels Mara was being a little sneaky with how she stood behind him and moved to maintain her proximity by pressing herself against his wings, peeking just over his shoulder.

"He got so aggressive all of a sudden." One of the women admitted. As they tried to explain Nanaeh would finally move to stand, the bleeding had finally stopped. He growled and stamped his foot on the ground as he moved forward to confront Pandora. The otter was now in front of the monk and looking down at him.

"You're gunna pay for this!" Nanaeh said while he pinched his nose closed with his hand, wincing at the pain talking caused. "You and your heretic!" The otter would storm off, eyes following him as he went. The black and white haired Rodrus would eventually follow, feeling that their pride was tattered in the process of helping Nanaeh. The other priests would look to Pandora to see his reaction, but were surprised to see he had turned to Mara and proceeded to check her over.

"Are you okay?" He didn't want to bring Mara here and put her into danger. Mara let him take her arm and look it over, a little smug he was checking to see if she was the one alright, even after she clobbered those three. She felt Pandora lean in close to her face as he moved to look into her eyes. "Why..." he whispered. "Why do you make me worry like that?" Mara shivered at the touch of his breath against her face.

"What are you gunna do, punish me?" Mara questioned, though that was indeed a thought. Pan tilted his head at her before stepping back. He turned to look at the gathered clergy and bowed his head.

"I'm sorry for the commotion." Pan apologized. Even the helpers who had witnessed the fight break out would call out to the monk. He hadn't done anything wrong. In fact he's been the most helpful one around since the start, they felt.

"Hey, hey don't be hard on yourself." One of the helpers spoke up. "Let's finish the lesson and send you guys off to the next one.

This time no animals. You'll be helping us clean up the Ranch." He expressed. The clergy shifted their attention. "Well it looks like master Frei is still not here, so he told us that if he took too long settling the Avius at the stalls, to take you to the edge of the Ranch by the lodge to help with clean up efforts." He explained. "See the miners come back every evening and stay at the lodge, but it can get messy when they spend the night so we have to clean up on the regular. With you all here you're going to be given brooms, mops, and laundry baskets to help clean everything up. You need to learn, as this will be a regular part of your life from now on. The churches can't afford slaves due to how funds are managed, so everything is done by volunteers or the clergy themselves." This didn't sit well with the spoiled priests as they called out in dismay. "Now, now. Let's get the Coursers back into the stalls and we'll go to the lodge." The clergy groaned, but would do as they were told.

Back at the homestead Shale was making his way out of the house, waving back to Mother Nal who clutched her apron with her free hand, bid the young man farewell and turned to head back into the house. As Shale climbed down the porch steps his rounded ears twitched before his head turned to follow a familiar sound.

"But Nanaeh... we aren't supposed to--" The black-haired goon tried to sooth the man's ire.

"Out of my way! I'll do what I want! I need to swim! Clear my head." And soothe his aching nose, but the running river was outside of the Ranch. The two goons came to a stop, a little afraid of leaving the gate. The two themselves were used to the comforts of the seminary academy so the thought of leaving out into the woods was scary. They would turn tail and run the other way. As for Shale he walked to the edge of the gate. The path led out to the woods and into the various roads the miners took. Some were marked, some were unmarked. Nanaeh went down the unmarked path towards the river. Being that the

Grassweaver and Reedwhistler families were quite outgoing and not as sheltered as most raised in a clergy's lifestyle, they knew the outdoors well.

Shale looked around and saw no one was about. Swallowing the lump in his throat Shale went to follow his uncle, wanting to talk to him while Nal's encouragement was still warm in his chest.

# CHAPTER TWENTY-ONE

## Why Would You...?

Nanaeh made his way down the dirt road. The wide road soon began to narrow into a rough trail. The area had rocky ground cover with soft, dark dirt that had been overgrown with moss and other native lichen. It was a rough, uneven forest floor that crossed by the very edge of the river. Young trees lined the length of the embankment with the tangled canopies dangling down to the average person's head height throughout the route. The water itself was somewhat murky and far from the clear bodies the otter was used to. The water was littered with smooth, colorful stones that had been carved by the rushing waters that bubbled up and frothed to a point that the edges of the river looked like dancing masses of sea cucumbers that had come ashore.

Nanaeh moved his hand from his nose, staring at his blood-stained palm. Grumbling, the man moved to step down from the edge of the stony floor, towards the water. The sound of footsteps called Nanaeh's attention. At first he assumed it was his two companions who finally grew some courage and made their way across the trial, but when Nanaeh turned his head to greet them with a snarky, upturned grin, he would instead see Shale standing under the dim lightning that washed down through the openings in the canopy above. He seemed to be standing far away, but he was much closer than he thought as when Shale stepped forward he was already at the edge of the river's bank. Nanaeh had already dipped his paw into the cool water, the other sitting on the bank. His thick tail was curled around a sapling that barely clung to the ground with its thin roots.

"Oh, it's you." Nanaeh's arms fell to his side as he responded to his unexpected company, flatly. "Why are you here? Shouldn't you be getting your boo boos checked out?" Nanaeh put his hands on his hips as he started to laugh. Shale pressed his paws together and nervously fidgeted. "Go away, can't you see I'm busy?" Though his nose had stopped bleeding he still had a throbbing headache. That woman had terrorized his face and attacked him multiple times in the head. As they stood amidst nature the wind would catch in the canopies, causing them to flutter. Shale looked up, hearing some movement in the brush. "Always such a coward, go back if you can't handle a little wind!"

"I-it isn't funny anymore Nanaeh!" Shale barked out. "You're always teasing me and causing me trouble!" Shale wouldn't back down this time. Nanaeh narrowed his eyes. He has had about enough of people talking back to him. He was strong and knew what he could get and what he couldn't. That woman wasn't above his league, if anything she was so far below it that the way he was having trouble was infuriating.

"It's you isn't it!?" Nanaeh pointed to Shale. The confused otter shirked, but tried his best not to step back. "Ash said there was gunna be some of you that would try and stop me. She's a heretic! It doesn't matter if I force her or she decides on her own!" Though Shale wasn't sure what Nanaeh was talking about, seeing as he wasn't trying to stop him from talking to the Drakus, even Shale could easily see that it wasn't right to harass the woman even if it was something allowed.

"Nanaeh, you can't force people to do things you want! If you keep this up you'll be punished by the goddesses!" Shale shouted, moving forward so that he was now but a few inches from Nanaeh. "If you keep this up someone'll stand up to you and you'll be sorry!" At his last, forceful shout Nanaeh perked his rounded ears. His brows pinched down into a scowl as he moved to step up out of the water. He pulled back his fist.

"That's enough out of you Shale!" Nanaeh was much bigger than Shale, over two heads. Nanaeh reached out and grabbed Shale's arm with his other hand, his fist coming down towards the smaller otter's face. Shale winched, shrinking away from the assault.

"No!" Shale shouted and threw out his paws, shoving them into the center of Nanaeh's chest. Shale lost his balance and fell backwards, hitting the hard ground. Shale wouldn't give Nanaeh the satisfaction and cry out in pain. Swallowing the feeling, Shale looked around. Nanaeh had stumbled forward, the sapling having been yanked from its roots at the harsh jerking of Nanaeh's tail. He had tightened his grip around the tree when Shale fell because he lost his footing on the wet stones. Webbed toes gripped the stones as Nanaeh climbed back onto the shore on his hands and knees. Reaching out he grabbed Shale by the ankle and pulled the young man close, swinging his fist down on his side, but again Shale wouldn't cry out.

"You mouthy little bastard!" Nanaeh's fist came down onto Shale again. "She's mine and I'm gunna beat the shit out of anyone who gets in my way!" Nanaeh continued to wail down on his nephew, taking out his frustrations on the younger man. Shale swallowed the pained cries at the edge of his lips, gasping out when he was struck in his head. Shale started to feel the stitches over his eyes burning. They began to bleed from the blunt force Nanaeh put on it.

Shale desperately looked around, paws grasping at the naked

forest floor, trying to pull himself away from Nanaeh's cloying, cruel paws. Shale managed to wrap his paw over a jagged stone and pull himself a bit away from Nanaeh, inching from the dangerous space. But suddenly, the larger otter pulled him back towards the water's edge. Nanaeh was able to get back onto his paws and moved to stand. Nanaeh grabbed Shale by his scruff with his left paw and spun him around. Nanaeh held his right paw up with his claws curled out as he moved to slash Shale across the face. Shale was pulled back, feeling the uncomfortable feeling of the skin and fur of his scruff being snagged and yanked around. When Shale was pulled to his feet he still had the stone in paw. He looked to the rock.

"Stop!" Shale shouted and spun around, slamming the stone up against the side of Nanaeh's head. He realized he hit his target and the paw around his scruff loossend. "Stop!" He raised his arm and slammed the stone down again and this time the hand left his body free. "Stop!" Shale shouted as the stone would come down again, the dull sound drumming in his ear with every strike. With this strike Nanaeh stepped back.

Again, again, and again.

With every hit Nanaeh seemed to retreat until finally the larger otter fell to his knees and was at eye level with Shale. Shale opened his eyes and stared at Nanaeh, face to face with his tormentor. Nanaeh's face was twisted, his nose and orbital bones broken to the point of deformation. His once bright eyes were now a distant, hazy color as they were unfocused. Shale didn't stop. His eyes were filled with ears and the stitched up wound over his eye was swelling, blocking the vision over his left eye. He would, once again, bring down the rock, slamming it across Nanaeh's face. Nanaeh didn't make a sound, but instead gagged up blood from his mouth before he fell backwards, his head slamming into the river stones below. The foamy waters would begin to wash away the blood from Nanaeh's face. his eyes trembling in pain. Shale dropped to his knees, pressing them onto Nanaeh's shoulders. Nanaeh slowly turned his eye to Shale who raised the blood spattered stone overhead with both paws and swung down.

The strike echoed so hard that it disturbed the gentle lull of the woods, causing a number of small animals to flee their hiding spots. Everything became quiet. The only sound that penetrated Shale's ears was the distant babbling of the river as it rushed across his thighs. He looked down where Nanaeh lay, motionless. The stone tumbled from Shale's hand and hit the river with a soft plunk, the waters cleaning the flecks of flesh and blood from the sharp stone's edges. Shale's chest rose and fell with his panting breaths. Nanaeh's eyes were open, but there was no consciousness behind his pupils. He wasn't breathing and his face looked as if it was mauled by a ravenous beast. Shale curled his lip, trying to speak, but no words would come.

A strangled noise rumbled from Shale's lips. He reached out to shake Nanaeh's shoulders, but there was no response. The rippling sound of croaking scratched from Shale's mouth as he tried to speak, tears falling from his face. No matter what Shale did, no matter how much he felt he called out, though no real words expressed from his lips, and no matter how much he tried to rouse him, Nanaeh did not respond. Shale pushed to his paws and turned to the riverbank. He pulled himself out of the cold water. His knees were scraped up, but because the water was so cold he couldn't feel anything. When Shale made his way onto shore he fell to his knees, hands reaching out as his body wanted to collapse. Opening his mouth to deny himself the reality, instead of the agonizing 'no' he wished to speak he would instead begin to vomit.

After emptying his stomach Shale walked back over to the river where Nanaeh lay in his back, arms splayed out and the water rushing across his lifeless body. Shale moved to stand beside Nanaeh, staring down at the man in silence. He raised his eyes, noticing something across the river. There were a pair of glowing eyes watching him. At first it was just one pair, then more eyes began to appear. Stepping from the shadows of the treeline was a pack of carnivorous hounds. They watched, soft growls rumbling from their bodies like the churning of empty stomachs.

"Look... look what you made me do, Nanaeh..." Shale finally found the will to talk, though he wasn't even sure if he was actually speaking aloud. "Now they're looking for you..." He stared at the beasts who cautiously stepped down into the waters. They would growl, threatening the young otter. The beasts facing Shale were a kind of wild hound typically found in the deep woods. They stood about waist height of the average man with thick, matted pelts that protected them against the cold rains that usually fell in the woods. This group had a mix of grey and gold coats with rounded ears and large, black socks on their paws. Their tails were fluffy and stood up as they tried making themselves look bigger in the face of this person.

Shale slowly stepped back and moved to climb back onto the embankment. He watched the beasts as they closed in on Nanaeh's body. Shale continued to back away and would make his way down the trail, back towards the Ranch. He could hear as the snarling beasts growled and feasted on the fallen form of Nanaeh. It was a sound Shale won't soon forget.

# CHAPTER TWENTY-TWO

## Family Traditions

After settling Ash in the Caper's sties, a helper on hand to show him how to handle the mischievous horned critters, Frei made his way back to the homestead to check in with his mother. After stitching Shale up, Nal — with her two daughters — worked on preparing supper. It was already early in the afternoon. The new contractors were probably already set upon the mines because the Wolus could hear the distant treble from the erupting explosives being used to clear the mountain paths. Upon entering the homestead, Frei removed his hat and would greet their mother and sisters.

"Oh, Frei," The mother spoke up, turning to face her older child. "You couldn't be done already for the day." She scooped up some of her apron and wiped her paws in the cloth, the girls turning to wave to their sibling before continuing their tasks. Nal walked over to Frei and reached up to rest her paws against their cheeks. She would check Frei over, turning their head to the side to check for any injuries. "Ya seem fine..."

"Because I am!" Frei assured her. "Just sent up a troublemaker to clean up the Capers and came to check on dad to see when the miners were coming down from the mountain. Figured he would be going up that way soon to drive you guys to deliver lunch." Normally it was his dad's job to escort his mother and sisters up the mountain to deliver the packed meals. It was something the miners got as a treat. Their hard work kept the mines open and their family prospering from the lands, so it was only right that Frei's family helped out in this way.

"Ah, you're right." Nal stated. "But we started lunch a lil late because your father is meeting a business partner at the docks. It was last minute so he asked us to start lunch a little late today." She turned back to the kitchen and walked over to the stove. It was a simple country kitchen with a stove top for cooking, an oven for baking, and a metal sink at the end for cleaning. Frei moved to the center of the room where a square, wooden island counter sat. Several cast iron pots hung above it with a few cutting utensils. Frei settled on the stool, their hand moving to rest on their thigh while they leaned their elbow on the counter. The Wolus had an uncomfortable look in their eyes.

"Pa didn't go to meet them, did they?" Frei wasn't sure who their father went to see, but they had an idea. There were few people they handled business with at the Ranch. "We got a good crowd today ma! I don't want those Slavers here to --" The sound of a knife coming down over the head of the fish that the mother Forestwalker was handling, sounded loudly through the room. The cleaver cut through the flesh and bones with ease. Frei found themselves threatened by the act and quickly silenced. They furrowed their brows and looked to the side, Frei's sisters quickly catching on as well and turned to hasten their tasks. "Ma --"

"Frei," Nal sighed. "I know you like them folk that come from abroad, but we have to think about our family. Your grandfather is struggling every day faring folk back and forth. He should be retired and relaxing in a rocker. Your brother is at the highest points prospecting almost every day. I hardly ever see him home any more, and you ask why? Frei, how else are we going to make enough money? Your sisters and I make those folk lunches everyday and see 'em. They're heretics. One of your cousins was already killed because of them refusing to follow rules. Besides, it's not like they're all going to be taken, just the ones that can't work in the mines and break the rules." She explained.

"Still..." Frei never liked the idea. "Shouldn't we at least wait until they've been here a few weeks first? Can't make assumptions on the first day." He never liked the idea of depending on the Slavers, but in some cases they would get more coin in a day for a few heretics than they could get in a week from the mines. Sometimes they were unlucky and the prospects they set up were dry, so they had to make up for the loss in profits. "We got some good priests this month and I think they'll be able to help us excavate the opal mine." At this Frei's mother turned to look towards them. "Some smart ones and strong fellows among them. I was gunna start training them early and take them up that way tomorrow." Frei only hoped it would be his chance to turn his father's thoughts away from helping the Slavers for a bit of extra coin.

"Really?" Nal said in interest. "Even your Pa's tried getting a priest from the mainland over there. It was haunted by some dreadful thing." She looked over to her daughters who stilled and slowly stopped their chore of stirring the great big pot of stew. "Why do you think this lot would do any better than the last ones? I heard the priests from the previous camp all quit after what it was they saw." The opal mine was a great find for the family, rare as well. Where red quartz was the most common find deep beneath the stony walls, coming upon other veins was rare. The opal mine could give them enough backing from the government on the mainland to develop their waterways and search for gem deposits in the rivers. "Well, alright. I'll trust you, but yer Pa will be bringing the Slavers ashore to act as guards and keep an eye on the miners. If any of them act up they won't be given a chance this time. Your Pa is still rightly upset from the last incident." Frei nodded in understanding. They wanted to give the heretics a chance at having normal jobs. A number of their permanent miners were heretics, but because they worked in the mines that profited the government and provided the red quartz geodes, they were allowed to work here under the watchful eye of the Forestwalker family.

While Frei carried on in their conversation with their mother, at the docks, a tall, brown-furred Wolus demi stood overlooking the ocean, watching a large, dark-colored boat make its way in. It was not a large vessel, by the standards of most, but this ship was designed to be fast in the water, to be able to get to the island and back its armada in a short time. By the flag being flown by the ship it was very clearly a Slaver's vessel. The Wolus frowned, his crossed arms tightening against his chest as he let out a shaky exhale. The demi had a short, fluffy tail and his paws were covered by leather boots. He wore a sleeveless tunic that was tucked into his grey trousers. On the Grani, old Varfri stood leaning over the side with his smoking pipe. The peg-legged captain stared down at the Wolfus demi. The man had dark skin and smooth hair that was combed back. His face was chiseled and his square jaw was clenched down as he tried to ignore the captain's gaze.

"You look nervous, Tyr." The old captain grinned, his fangs biting down on the stem of the pipe. A soft smoke billowed up, out of the bowl. The contents were a simple collection of tobacco and herbs and gave the smoke a calming sensation that soothed the nerves and took care of some minor aches as to be expected from regularly riding the icy waves of the northern seas. "That ships getting close. Picked out anyone yet--?"

"Please!" Tyr barked out. The demi turned to look at the older kin. He let his arms fall to his sides as he allowed the frown previously playing at the corners of his lips to fully overcome his expression. "Dad, please." Tyr begged. "I know it isn't ideal, but cause of them Uggi is dead." His nephew, like many of his side of the family, worked on the island. Uggi was his nephew and Frei's cousin. Because of a couple of heretics starting a fight over a resource node they had tried to hide, Uggi ended up in the middle of their fight and died.

"You know that's a damn excuse. You been giving up those boys out there since long before Uggi. How many men ye got sold off, Tyr? You gotta take some responsibility for that." Vafri pressed his son. "I don't trust them." He reached his paw up to his pipe and removed it. "Slavers may have government identifiers, but they're still heretics themselves. Something about selling your own kind just doesn't sit right with me." Tyr frowned at his father.

"Our family used to be heretics too, dad." Tyr reminded him. There was a time, long ago, that they were nothing but heretics to the people of the mainland. It was exhausting to always have this kind of discussion with his father. They were doing what they could to survive in the world. It wasn't always easy to keep such fertile land to one self. Kokivorosdos Island was a paradise in the sea where many of the islands on Tier were not suitable for living on. After gaining their identification from the government the Forestwalker pack had settled on Kokivorosdos and turned the dry soils with their own paws. Because they tilled the land they were allowed to claim it for their clan, but most of what they discovered there was considered a resource that was owned by the government. They were expected to sell their resources for profit and encouraged to raise animals and expand out from their small Ranch. By now they had cultivated almost half of the island, the other half still untamed woodland.

"Don't you forget what we did boy." Vafri warned. "We didn't hunt folk for this land. We worked it with our own backs. Bah!" The old captain complained. "You better watch it. A heretic girl traveled in with the priests. She ain't with the miners and contractors. That's Frei's responsibility so don't you interfere with the pup!" With that Vafri stepped down from his perch and went into his ship, his crew wincing when the door to the captain's quarters slammed.

Finally the Slaver's ship would dock. From the now anchored boat stepped a black-furred Wolus kin. He had the usual uniform expected of the Slavers, including a leather harness over a dark tunic. He wore grey trousers and had a pair of leather sandals over his paws. Walking with him down the gangplank were a few Rodrus kin who were dressed differently. If one didn't know any better they looked like simple workers with their red or blue tunics and tan pants. He folded his arms behind his back and he would smile.

"I am guessing you are ser Tyr?" The Slaver spoke. "I'm Oaker. I'll be assisting with the collection." From a space on the Grani a pair of eyes studied Tyr and Oaker...

# CHAPTER TWENTY-THREE

## It's A Bad Memory

After airing out his concerns and his mother's reassurances, Frei would return to the stables to check on things. With the helpers' assistance the priests were able to put back the Coursers. Seeing that everything was in place Frei would start his way towards the lodge where they were likely at by this point. The helpers were able to get all the priests to the lodge and had them in groups, cleaning up their areas. Downstairs in the lodge some of the training clergy were sweeping and picking up discarded bottles of ale while others were in the kitchen cleaning dishes. On the second floor, where the bedrooms were located, there were a few beds that needed the linen collected from them in order to be cleaned. After the rooms were cleared of trash the rest would start on clearing the bedding.

"Mara please..." Pandora somehow got paired up with Mara which made him a little suspicious as to the helper's intentions. Did they want him to finish tasks or not? While normally he worked well, quickly, and efficiently, Mara seemed to have it out for him, distracting him from his work. "Do you really want such a thing?" Not that he wasn't curious nor uninterested in

Mara's suggestion. The Drakus had laid herself on the bare bed, as they had removed the old bedding, leaving the mat exposed. She had laid herself on her back, her thick, draconic tail lazily swaying between her raised knees. The hem of her dress covered anything untoward, like a curtain drawn over her knees.

"Aren't you curious?" Mara questioned. "I noticed you looking." She tugged up the skirt, easing the fabric over her knees as she watched Pandora's reaction. He hadn't taken his eyes off the spot. The location between her thighs with markedly different looking scales interested Pandora for a while. He was curious and it was difficult for him to ignore that touch of neuroticism that was unique to him. Pandora felt his feathers ruffle as it was revealed to him. A magnificent vision of scales that he had only seen from afar up until this point. Pandora approached the Drakus and moved to rest a knee on the mat. Leaning close he looked down at Mara who stared up at him with questioning eyes. His hesitation made her nervous. When Pandora reached out she tensed up slightly, her knees coming together as she watched him.

"Do you want I look, or not?" The woman seemed beside herself with the decision. He moved to rest his hand on her knee, but that was enough to get her to relax. He moved to part her legs and looked over the scales in question. They were unlike the ones on her body. They were wider, rectangular in shape, and seemed to have a sheen that was lighter than the cerulean diamonds that covered her body. "I'm going to touch them..." When Mara turned her head away he hesitated, but since the Drakus kept her legs apart it encouraged the Avius to move forward and touch his fingers to the specialized scales. They were indeed soft to the touch, but did he prefer the soft scales? "I like all your different scales, Mara." They were all good, he decided. The hard ones were fun to touch, the soft ones were as well. They were nice and his favorite color. He traced his fingers along the line of ventral scales, tracing up between her legs before finding that the entire space was soft and inviting.

He curled his finger up, curious at the folds of fat that seemed incorporated into the flesh. Mara quickly tensed up and folded her legs together, trapping his arm.

Just in that moment the bedroom's door would open. One of the helpers peeked their head in. "Ya'll done in here?" When he looked around Mara was sitting up in the bed with her hands resting on her knees and Pandora was seated on the bed's edge, on his knees. The Avius looked back to the door, then to the sack full of laundry.

"Yes, shall we bring it down?" Pandora moved to step up from the bed and walked over to the bloated sack. He kneeled down before standing, hoisting the bag over his shoulder. The helper motioned his paw and turned to leave, confirming to Pandora his next step. Pan looked back at Mara as she slid off the bed. Her face was still a little red and she brushed down the hem of her dress. The helper left the room, leaving the two to their own devices. Mara moved to walk up to Pandora's side. She felt as if his fingers were still on her scales. Squeezing her legs together she felt her cheeks heat up as the blood rushed to her head from the thoughts. "Mara, did I go too far?" She felt he hadn't gone far enough.

"N-no. It's fine." He had explored her scales and anywhere his fingers could reach between her thighs. She had almost fainted at the sensations. She didn't think she could feel so much under his touch, under anyone's really. "You can -- feel them again when you want to." Pandora looked to Mara's face, tilting his head. He considered her offer. It seemed a little intimate.

"Do you want me to?" He asked. The Drakus looked to Pandora as if he spat out a curse. Her cheeks were red and that heavy tail beat against the ground most aggressively. He tried to bite back the smirk, only to fail. "Well if that's what you want. I wouldn't mind. I like your scales. All of them." He turned to leave the room. Mara jumped up and hurried to follow him out, but as they left the room there was a bit of a commotion downstairs.

When they looked over the banister from the second floor, down to the first, Frei looked to have entered! The rancher removed his hat and pressed it to his chest.

"I see everyone's workin' hard!" Frei was glad to see that. They stood at the entryway of the lodge before glancing back at their guest. Frei made a bothered expression before he sighed and looked ahead. "Hey, all. So we got a guest from the mainland. They'll be helping us with some work later as they're experienced with maintaining the mining tools. Let me introduce ya'll to Oaker!" From behind the Wolus stepped another, though this fellow was black-furred kin as opposed to a demi like Frei. He seemed to be wearing a simple white, long-sleeved tunic with grey pants. He had a bandolier across his shoulder and a belt around his waist that had a heavy satchel, hatchet, and a whip. "He'll be helping us with our last task for the day and our tasks tomorrow." The kin stepped forward and pulled back his muzzle in a dark grin. Inside his mouth were sharp, predatory teeth, but he appeared to be missing his upper, right canine.

"Ayo kids. I'm Oaker. Don't let my grey fur fool you, I'm still pretty young and sturdy." He reached up to scratch at the greying fur just beneath his chin. At the top of the steps Pandora stared down at the black-furred kin who stepped in behind Frei. The other priests approached, greeting the tall, handsome man. But for Pandora this was a nightmare.

"Pan?" Mara noticed something was bothering the Avius and turned to look at him, reaching up to grab his arm before pulling it towards her, squeezing it between her chest. "You look a little pale." She tried to pull him close to her body. Was it something she had done? Maybe she didn't respond enough for his taste. Pandora shook his head, staring down at the man below.

"That man...." Pandora was focused on the kin covered in black fur with some grey patches under his chin and along the back of his ears. "He should be dead." Now Pan wasn't the sort of person to wish others dead but he would swear to the goddesses that this man -- he had seen him dead somewhere. Pandora took a step back, dropping the sack to the floor. At the sound Frei and some of the others looked up towards the top of the stairs.

"Oh, an' that little fella is our visiting Oikos monk. He'll be helpin' out same as everyone else. Hey fella, why don'tcha come down here an' say hello to our guest?" Frei wanted to make sure Oaker could recognize the monk and his follower. He didn't want this guy to mistakenly take them thinking they were the miners. As far as Frei knew Slavers didn't even care to check the clothes a person wore before taking them without thought, only ever thinking of their profits.

"No...." Pan took a step back, his arm sliding from Mara's grip. His back pressed against the wall as he slid down to the ground.

"*Pan*?!" Mara called, but her voice seemed far away.

"*Oy? What happened to Pandora*?!" Frei was the first to come running up the steps when they noticed the haunted expression on the Avius' palling face as he stumbled back.

*Pan! Pan --* ***Derrick run***!

# CHAPTER TWENTY-FOUR

## A Dark Night

**AAUUUUUUUUEEEEGH**

The sound of screams sang through the night like a chorus of suffering. No one knew what was going on, confusion having become a strangely familiar companion. Fires had broken out throughout the jungle turning the once deep blue night into a hellish crimson red. Strange, black furred men had invaded their village, like shadows, boogeymen on the hunt for the lives of the innocents, to steal them from their beds. The whips and chains that they carried in their hands cracked through the air like a thunderstorm. They were monsters because they didn't fight like men. They used their claws, they used their teeth, and even some of them used their bodies to cut scars, pain, and suffering into everyone they passed. What had gone wrong...? Everything was peaceful but an hour ago...

It had been only an hour since the people of the village had gone to bed. They all lived in tree houses that were intricately braided into the canopies, the huts wrapped around the tree's trunk like mushrooms, looking as if they were naturally formed in the wood by way of stripped bark, woven bamboo, and braided reeds. Rope bridges and slat walkways extended from each hut across the paths filling out the village's shape based on the grove of trees. Torches were perched at the sides of the bridges and along the more important huts during the day, but at night they were all put out for safety. Come that night it was business as usual. All fires had been put out, leaving nothing but the gleam of the twin moon's light and curtain of stars above lighting the dense jungle overgrowth that sheltered the homes hidden amongst the leaves. The soft light of the moons painted a bright shine onto the blue and violet leaves below, leaving the surrounding jungles to give off a natural, blue glow.

Tomorrow's chores would usually consist of families collecting water for the reservoir, food being hunted and foraged for, as well as building of new huts or maintenance of older ones. But tomorrow would never come for the village, for the shadows arrived. The hunters swooped in like demons and set their beautiful home ablaze.

~ ~ ~ ~ ~

"Encircle the grove, make sure no one can get out!" A large Wolus howled at his companions. He was a large demi with black fur. His eyes were a soft brown and his paws were protected by leather wraps. Around his chest he wore a harness with a whip with chains and manacles hooked against his belt. His deep, tan sarouel trousers were tightly wrapped at the ankles with white swathing cloth to protect his legs from the thorny underbrush of the jungle. He was tall and had black ears with white patches along the back that looked like eye spots. The underside of his muzzle, down to his chest, was a white patch of fur that stood out against his natural charcoal coat. The man didn't come alone and had brought with him a massive pack of over twenty individuals who worked to overwhelm the tiny village.

The black-furred Slavers had invaded promptly. After months of preparation and searching they were able to locate the village within the jungle. It took picking apart clues and following the word of mouth from travelers to finally discover the invisible world outside the borders of what was considered land protected by the goddesses. This made anyone living outside these borders natural heretics and looked down on by everyone else. Though they were known as Slavers as a whole, this gang in particular was known as the Skuggi. The man currently in charge was Oaker Griefbringer. He stood with a hatchet in hand, having been at the head of the second party cutting through the thick wall of foliage that barred their way.

"Master Oaker," One of the young Slavers would call out. Oaker turned his head to the black furred kin that walked up to his side. He appeared to be about twenty years of age, having already been an adult for four of those years. The pup should have already been brought into the field for his training. "Shouldn't we have done this in the day?" Normally they did their raids during the early evening or morning. His concern was understandable, but more so his ability to recognize that something was different about this hunt.

Oaker smirked and moved his hand down to the young man, resting it on the small of his back. "Today is special because we're after a type of heretic thought to have long gone extinct come the end of the era." He reached out his hand as the first fires started to be lit. "This is the only known place where the black-winged Avius can be found. It'll be unknown soon enough and we'll have captured every last one of them. At least the ones that survive the smoking."

The other Slavers of the groups had taken strategic points around the jungle habitat and lit fires in order to force the inhabitants into a chokepoint. At this point in time the villagers were still sound asleep, unaware of the terror that awaited them.

Among the numerous huts a small boy was sitting out on the gangplank just outside of his hut. He looked to be a young demi with pale ash talons and a thin frame. He looked to be no older than four or five and wore a long, white tunic with black trousers. His little claws grasped the vines of the walkway with casual ease while his hands rested on the tops of his thighs.

"Derrick?" A woman called in a soft voice. The boy looked back towards the woman. She was a tall demi with thick, black plumage that was as dark as an abyss. The edges of her feathers seemed to glisten with a sheen of green and purple. She had luxuriously thick wings and a long beak that curved ever so slightly at the end, but it was otherwise straight and a sleek, black color as was much of the rest of her. What stood out were her green eyes that matched the little boy's. She wore a bright blue embroidered tunic with gold colored trim. Around her hips was a sky blue sash that held up white sarouel trousers. Reaching down, her wings spread out to wrap around the fledgling, scooping him up into the cradle of black. "What are you doing up so late? Couldn't sleep?" The boy giggled and settled back against her wings, looking up to the sky.

"Mm." The boy grunted and continued to stare into the sky. He had been watching the moons. "I was asking the moons a question." The boy curled his feet together, talons clasping one another as he moved to grab his ankles with his hands. "But they're not answering. Do you know mama?" The woman looked down to the young boy and tilted her head.

"What did you ask them?" She wondered. "You know the goddesses don't always answer directly to you. You have to use the special stones." Derrick scrunched up his face and shook his head. His mother chuckled. "Alright, what did you want to ask them?" She lowered her head, placing her ear hole close to him. The boy turned his head up to her and giggled.

"Why is the sky always pink and red?" He had always wondered why the pink sky was filled with orange-red clouds that looked as if they were painted on the ceiling above, but at night those red-orange rays fell to the horizon and hung there like a halo leaving the night sky a deep pink, almost magenta that dulled the senses and made one sleepy. But before his mother could answer a whistle rang through the village.

"**FIRE**!" A voice echoed through the village. The darkness within the huts began to brighten as lanterns were lit and people hurried awake. The woman leaned down and looked along the forest floor noticing the flames that were lit up in different patches of foliage. The flames were unnaturally placed around and gave her a sense of unease. She would continue to search the shadowy shapes along the trees looking for what had everything amiss. There she would see some of the figures below attempting to sneak away from their posts towards their rendezvous positions. "Derrick, go wake your father." She remained calm, setting her offspring down on the bridge.

"Okay!" The small bird ran into his family's hut. His mother followed behind in a hurry, but she took care to retain her calm. Derrick ran into his parent's room where his father slept in the bed. "Papa!" He jumped onto the man's belly, starting him awake. The man jerked forward, curling his legs, arms reaching out from beneath the covers. He coughed out and looked over to his son, the boy giggling and bouncing on the older male's belly. When he realized he was alone in bed he looked around before he caught his wife's movement across the room, in the hallway. She looked at the demi male as his face twisted up in confusion. The woman put her finger to her beak before she hurried into the children's room where Derrick's bed was and the baby's bassinet. Wrapping up the baby she stepped out of the room. He would finally climb out of bed, quickly tossing on a shirt that was hanging off a chair. As he moved to stand he would pick up the young boy and carry Derrick out into the main area of the hut, perched in his arm.

"What's going on?" The older Avius asked in a whisper. He had on a lapis colored tunic with white trousers. Unlike his wife's more ornate top his was more plain, but did not lack decoration as various designs were carved into the leather stitching around the collar, sleeves and hem of his shirt. The woman hurried passed him towards the hut's exit. He followed his wife as she hurried out and moved along the walkways. He noticed their neighbors were rushing out their huts, clutching their young close to their bodies or hustling along with a sack of belongings. "Danger?" He raised his nose in the air, noticing the thick scent of smoke. "Fires?"

"People." She corrected him. "I saw them lighting the fires, but I don't know who they are or what they're here for." She rushed towards a ladder which led down to the forest floor. She moved to swaddle the baby around her chest and began climbing down. Her husband pulled Derrick onto his back before he turned to follow the woman. "We need to go." She maintained a low tone and quickly arrived at the bottom of the rope ladder before hopping off, stepping back as her husband quickly followed suit. As the villagers began to escape from the fires the Slavers moved around in order to round them up.

"Don't let any of them escape! If they aren't writhing from the smoke, chain them up!"

**AAUUUUUUUUEEEEGH**

The cracks of metal and the snap of whips were followed by the sounds of agony, roaring through the once sleeping jungle.

# CHAPTER TWENTY-FIVE

## Breaking Apart

"Run!" The sound of Derrick's father called out in the dense jungle. Their footfalls were almost silent against the pounding backdrop of screams and heavy combat. Some of the black-feathered Avius had decided to fight back, but others were instantly captured in the metal chains the Slavers were so fond of. These steel chains were nothing like the iron or leather harnesses that were easily worn and broken through with the right amount of force. In the past it took two or more Slavers to capture a target and strap them properly in a harness, or lock up the iron manacles with a hefty ring of keys that weighed down on the Slavers. The recent innovation of steel manacles and rivets made it easier for Slavers to lock down their targets and take them back to the ship without worry of them running free. With this the men only needed to tighten a single bolt, leaving other Slavers to move around independently to make their capture. Those caught were dragged back to the vessel and those who couldn't escape the fire in time died.

Oaker marched through the flames, cutting away the vegetation to keep the fires controlled and away from him and his men's path. The young Wolus watched as the man seemed to effortlessly handle the fire, unafraid of the heat or sparks. He had a mask pulled over his muzzle to protect him from the smoke. The young man also had a mask and carried a machete that he used to break through the wild herbage that seemed to curl back in after being torn to shreds, as if it were alive. Soon he came to the edge of the perimeter they had made. Oaker perked his ears and realized there were some openings in their net. That was problematic. That would mean less money for them if too many got away, especially the children and newborns that were said to have been spotted among the droves of heretics during previous observations. There was a man in the south looking for these slaves and was willing to pay in advance for the Skuggi pack to hunt them down. This curious collector had been the one to fund their expedition in the first place, claiming the Avius were an extinct subset of Tieran that no longer existed outside or within any territory. The promise of extra pay for every other Avius captured alive and brought in only served to sweeten the pot and increase their prey drive.

"Stop..." Oaker reached down to rest his paw on the young Wolus' shoulder. When the boy turned to face him Oaker would hand him a set of chains. "You head that way and make sure no one's gone through that opening. I'll come up this way to pick off any stragglers." He patted the young man's back to send him off. The boy went down the west path which looked to have been burned out. The fire had run out of fuel to follow as the path opened into a clearing, leaving the grove. Oaker followed the eastern path where the fire just couldn't catch against the moisture heavy environment.

"This way!" Derrick's mother called to her husband who held the young boy clutched to his chest. The mother was crouched down in some bushes a few feet ahead, waving her hand, beckoning to him. The bushes in question led through an opening in the firewall. It led out towards a clearing that guided the village towards the river. If they could get to the water they could wade across and make it through before the hunters caught their scent. "Stay low." She warned him.

"Daddy?" The boy murmured, looking up to his father while the older raven Avius remained crouched. His little legs were wrapped around his torso while his hands clutched to the front of his shirt. The man smiled, moving his finger to his lips, supporting the boy by his bottom with his hand. The boy opened his mouth in a little gasp before pulling his little hands over it, sealing his lips. Though it was a little scary with the fires all around, his parents were staying quiet and leaving so he was sure they knew what they were doing and it was best to follow them and copy what they did. The older male moved to stand under the shade of the massive tree he crouched beside and took a step to follow after his wife.

~CAHCHT!~

"Augh!" Derrick's father shouted out in pain as the tail-end of the whip snapped against his back with such precision that it tore a diagonal rip across the back of his tunic. The man glanced back to see a young Wolus had caught up to them. "Derry, run to mom okay?" He set the boy down. Derrick looked back to his father and hesitated. "Don't worry, I'ma fight the bad guy, but I can't if Derry's here." Derrick would nod and turn to run across the field. The Wolus noticed the little fledgling scurrying across the clearing toward the arms of a waiting woman. If he let too many get away, Oaker would scold him.

"That's enough from you!" The Wolus quickly grabbed the chains from his waist and snapped the manacle around the man's wrist before forcibly yanking him to the ground. Derrick's father let out a surprised shout when he was suddenly pulled forward. He stumbled to the ground, only for the Wolus to slam his whip down on him. Thinking quickly he would use the tree to his advantage. Throwing the length of the chain around the trunk he would catch the cuff of the second manacle. He snapped the fetter around the man's other wrist and locked him up against the tree. Without wasting time he kicked off the ground and rushed toward the young boy that had gotten a head start.

"Run!" Derrick's father shouted across the clearing. The boy's mother would look up as she held out her arms, reaching for him. She looked up past Derrick and would see the Wolus chasing him down, quickly catching up. The woman moved to stand and rushed towards the fierce looking predator. She spread out his wings in a threatening manner as she stepped in front of Derrick. The Wolus didn't stop and pulled back his whip, but he hadn't expected the kick straight to his chest. He was thrown to the ground, grunting in surprise. The woman crouched down and would remove the swaddle from her around herself before wrapping the baby up tight around the young boy.

"Derrick, run to the river, and don't stop!" She warned.

"But mama!" The woman forcibly turned him around.

"Go!" Though hesitant to leave his parents, he knew the way to the river as he often accompanied his mother to collect water. Taking a few steps away he turned to run. Looking back he would see as the Slaver sat up and turned his head to the side to spit the blood from his muzzle, his mask having been pulled aside in the scuffle. Pulling his lips back into a growl revealed that he had lost a canine tooth in the struggle. "I'm your opponent!" The woman shouted, realizing he was focused on her son still. She balanced on a foot and snapped her left talon around his throat, choking the slaver before slamming him to the ground once more. She would hammer his body on the ground over and over, blood running from his mouth and a snap sounding as she pinned him down and jammed her beak into his throat.

"Get her!" Another voice sounded from the treeline as two more Slavers showed up and rushed out to help their comrade. The two men struggled but they managed to get a manacle around her ankles and pulled her to the ground. "Is he okay?"

"Doesn't matter, she got his throat. He'll be dead soon." He reached around his harness to pull a cloth from the bandolier before he lit it with a spark lighter. Waving the handkerchief in the air he would signal to the others in the village before throwing the cloth down by the fallen Wolus' body. Fires quickly rose from the smoldering kerchief. Flames picked up and closed up the wall of fire they had made. They quickly worked to unchain Derrick's father from the tree and dragged the fighting woman along with them. From the edge of the river the small boy would watch as the flames consumed the fallen Slaver and his mother and father were taken away.

"What about that way? Some escaped to the river!" The Slavers howled across the air, communicating commands.

"Go get them! Flush them out with smoke!" There was nothing but a waterfall that way so they would have nowhere to go. Upon hearing this Derrick gasped and spun around, but in his panic he failed to look where he was going and stumbled over a rock before he fell forward and into the river.

An adult could easily stand in the waist high waters, but a small boy didn't stand a chance in the rushing river. Derrick struggled to keep his head above water, flailing his arms in a panic. As he struggled the swaddle became loose and the wrapped baby slipped from his tiny body. The infant began to cry, matching her brother's shouts as they were drenched in the icy liquid. Soon those cries became dull hums. The roar of the waterfall that they were washed towards became deafening. When the Slavers finally reached the waters edge with their torches and looked around, there was nothing to find. Derrick and the infant had gone over the falls and vanished into the dark waters below...

# GLOSSARY

**Demi** - Tieran who have more hominid features with some animal features

**Kin** - Tieran who share more features with beast or anthropomorphic people

**Therion** - unnatural shapes taking during lunar changes

**Er-** Deadly Therion shapes that often increase strength and reduce intelligent thought

**Ti-** A subdued Therion shape that increases strength slightly and doesn't alter intelligence

**Heka'terra** - Silver Moon, Goddess of Magic

**Sele'terra** - Red Moon, Goddess of Stars

**Agro'terra** - Sun, Goddess of Destruction

**Oikos** - Monastic religion of communal living, means Moon

**Artimmus** - Cult-like religion of independent living, Means 'short time'

**Kreais kent** - old word for meat hunter, modern word for raider or bandit

**Oion** - old word for egg

**Kosos** - old word meaning to shine

**Avius** - Avian people of Tieran

**Porcinus** - Pig-like people of Tieran

**Mustus** - Musteline-like people of Tieran

**Felius** - Feline-like people of Tieran

**Wolus** - Wolf-like people of Tieran

**Drakus** - Dragon-like people of Tieran

**Gnolus** - Hyena-like people of Tieran

**Salmandrus** - Amphibious people of Tieran

**Vertebrus** - Insect-like people of Tieran

**Rodrus** - Rodent-like people of Tieran

**Ursus** - Bear-like people of Tieran

**Fius** - Fish-like people of Tieran

**Cetophus** - Octopus & Cuttlefish-like people of Tieran

**Equus** - Horse-like people of Tieran

**Saurus** - Reptilian people of Tieran

**Bovus** - Bovine-like people of Tieran

**Proyus** - Racoon-like people of Tieran

**Arachus** - Arachnid-like people of Tieran

**Cetus** - Whale-like people of Tieran

**Viverrus** - Civet-like people of Tieran

# ABOUT THE AUTHOR

**R.a. Rex Draco**

I am an Illustrator and writer who has been in love with storytelling since we were a wee dragon. I am a member of the furry community with friendships within the LGBTQ+ community so I understand the need for being inclusive and as such these are often represented in my stories as part of my greater worldbuilding. I write comics, light novels, and other types of unique genre models that represent myself and the communities I am part of.

I love science fiction first and foremost, romance, action and monster stories so those are usually the primary genres I focus on with subgenres focus such as Adventure, War, Romantic Comedy, Historical & Dramatic Romance, Psychological, and Heist/Crime stories. Please look forward to my work and I hope everyone has a day~!

# THANK YOU

Thank you for purchasing this book. I will soon have more to this series and other series posted up on Amazon and Books2Read. If you're interested in supporting the xVerse series and my other comic properties check out my Patreon or donate to my Ko-Fi. Thanks again for your purchase. Please leave a review if you enjoyed it!

www.ingramcontent.com/pod-product-compliance
Lightning Source LLC
LaVergne TN
LVHW010946110826
845149LV00015B/3229
*9798990466524*